THE ANCHOR

A Christian Historical Novel

BETHEL SERIES – BOOK 3

Tabbie Chamberlain

Copyright © Tabbie Chamberlain

All rights reserved. No part of this book may be copied or reprinted except in the case of quotations for special articles, reviews and inspirational thoughts in which case author must be noted. Biblical names and scriptures are taken from the Holy Bible, King James Version.

1872 America/France History-fiction, Christian Romance-fiction, Suspense-fiction

Cover picture: New Africa/stockadobe.com/licensed
"The Spider and the Fly" (Mary Howitt 1799-1888)

Where real-life historical figures appear, situations, incidents, and dialogues concerning those persons are fictional and are not intended to portray actual happenings. All other characters are the author's own imagination and any resemblance to actual persons are not intended. Dialogues of historical events relating to real situations are fictional and belong solely to the author. Although some of the descriptive historical art and architect are true, dialogue belongs to the author. This is a work of fiction. The author, therefore, makes no claims or warranties as to quality or accuracy of historical figures and events. The author, by no means, intends discrimination, prejudice, or criticism against any social, cultural, ethnic, creed or location.

Library of Congress Control Number: 2024945199

ISBN:
eBook: 979-8-89496-838-4
Paperback: 979-8-89496-831-5
Hardcover: 979-8-89496-830-8

Published in Orlando, US

Also by Tabbie Chamberlain

Inspirational: When I Sit In Darkness

Christian Historical Fiction:

Bethel Series:

BETHEL (Book 1)

GLIMMER of HOPE (Book 2)

In loving memory of my husband,

Samuel Hershal Chamberlain

April 7, 1934 – October 29, 2017

THE ANCHOR

Will your anchor hold in your darkest night,
When the storms of life are crashing?
When anguish and grief banish the light,
And turbulent waters are dashing.
Will your anchor hold when tidal waves of pain
Have stolen your will to live?
Will your anchor hold while fighting angry billows
Until you've no more strength to give?
When the piercing winds of heartbreak
Have left you barren and cold,
Are you secured to the Rock of Ages?
The Anchor that will hold.

(TC,2023)

1872
Prologue

Leaning on his staff, the aged gentleman, with eyes transfixed on the eastern sky, stood mesmerized by the beauty of the gorgeous sunrise. The expression on his countenance seemed to reflect the splendor that held him captive. With stooping shoulders from a debilitating infirmity that had taken its toll over the years of hard work and heavy lifting, he was still an imposing figure of size and dignity. Aged, but not considered a really old man at sixty-five, many years had passed since he first came to live at this peaceful place. Of the more than two thousand acres, he actually owned only one. It was a gift from his master.

Watching the sun as it slowly moved above the horizon, he reflected on when first coming to the plantation. The aged gentleman smiled as memories flooded him.

My sweetheart wuz already heah. She worked fer de Missus befo she come to de plantation. After de Missus married de Mastah, she come wit' de Missus and been heah evah since. I come to de plantation looking fer work and de Mastah hired me, and din I married dat purtty little gal dat wuz ten years my young'r. Sometimes I's still don't know why she married an ole man like me. I sho is grateful she did, and we's took on de Mastah's name and belonged to him. Dey nevah treated us like we wuz slaves but like we wuz part of de family. Dey gave us a house to live in and have kept it up all des years and added to it as de young'uns come along. And today, we's still heah, and dey sho do take good care of us. Who could ask fer anthin' moe.

With a slight quiver in his voice and while not quite as strong as it once was, the old gentleman spoke clearly. "Well, dat sun is gitting high'r and high'r and my missus be already to de big house stirring up some mornin' grub. Guess I's better mosey on dat away."

Somewhat wobbly and using the walking stick as a precaution, he started down the path that led from his house to the stables and blacksmith shop. "I's made dis journey many a day. Iffen I's only had a penny fer evah step I's taken on dis very path, I sho would be a rich man." He chuckled. "Os, but ye is rich ole man. All de money in dis ole world can't nevah buy what ye have. God has sho blessed ye wit' a good family and a good house. We's nevah lacked fer any o' dis life's needs. De Mastah made sho o' dat. He nevah claimed to own us. He always say we be free. Befoe de law say we free, we already be free."

The aged man continued down the path. Although not as strong and sturdy physically as he once was, he was stalwart in spirit with an unshakeable dependability. The master could count on his stability. No one could call him wimpy. A little feeble, yes, but never wimpy.

The old man smiled, knowing he was being followed. It was not necessary to look back, for the one trailing him was the one who followed him almost every day. Although quite a bit smaller than he, the little shadow took every step he did with many skips and hops in between since her small legs could not stretch the distance his long limbs could. He stopped walking. She stopped walking. The little follower did not want him to know she was dogging his trail, so he pretended not to know. He took a few steps forward. She took a few steps forward. Continuing at a slow pace, he glanced back knowing that she was not watching him but was looking down so as not miss a step. As the habit was, the leader stopped, turned and released a chuckle. The follower stopped with both small feet inside one of his large footsteps.

"I's waitin'. Come on, Lennie Sarah. Come take Pappy's hand and let's go de rest of de way together."

The little girl ran as fast as her small legs would carry her and threw her short arms around his legs. "I love ye, Pappy Moses. I love ye so much."

The aged man's eyes filled with tears and he picked up the child. "I's love ye, Lennie Sarah. I's sho do. Ye are one o' Pappy's many blessings. In fact, ye are at de top o' dis ole man's list o' blessings."

"Pappy Moses, ye are not ole. Ye be just my Pappy. I don't nevah want ye to git ole and die."

He squeezed her tight. More to himself than to her, he said, "Great wuz de day dat Fancy and Ephraim blessed Pappy Moses and Mammy Zip with such an angel. God sho did smile on us dat day." Putting her firmly on the ground, he took her hand and together they continued on the path to the blacksmith shop.

"Pappy," Lennie Sarah asked, looking up at him, "does it hurt walking with a stick?"

"No, baby, it don't hurt none. Just gives me somethin' to lean on."

"Ye can lean on me. I's strong, uh, I mean I'm strong. You can hold on to me, Pappy."

Moses smiled, looking down at the small girl. "Ye shorely is strong. Ever'body needs somethin' or someone to lean on, to hold on to."

At the shop, Moses went about his duties as Lennie Sarah bombarded him with endless questions. He never grew tired or impatient with her constant chattering. It was like music to his ears.

"What's this, Pappy?"

Moses stopped what he was doing and walked over to her. "What's what, baby?"

She pointed. "This big old iron thing with a ring at the top of a pole and two sharp funny looking arms sticking out from the bottom."

"Dat, Lennie Sarah, tis an anchor."

"Pappy Moses, what's an anchor?"

The aged gentleman looked at the anchor and patted the top of the little girl's head, his snarled fingers feeling the mass of curly hair beneath them. "Well…. an anchor tis solid and firm." Staring into space, he spoke barely above a whisper. "Tis like de Lawd. T'will hold ye steady when de storms of life come yo way. When de winds of grief and pain shake ye and rock ye to de very soul. When de angry billows beat ye down til ye feel like ye can't git up. He be dat one ever'body can lean on and hold on to."

He felt two small hands wrap around his large one. "So, Pappy Moses, if everything and everybody need something to hold on to and to lean on, is an anchor like a pillar? Like the pillars at Bethel on the front of the big house? It looks to me like the big pillars are holding it up. They look strong to me, and I figure if something happened to them, the big house would crumble down on top of Mastah Sam and Missus Tabitha and Little Dove."

Moses looked down into eyes as dark as midnight but shining like stars. "Well, Lennie Sarah, in some ways a pillar tis like an anchor. Dae is usually built to last a long, long time, strong and sturdy. Ye is right. Dem big pillars tis a holding up de verande' roof of de big house. Unlike de anchor, ye can see de pillars. Dae is very purtty and pleasant to de eye, very smooth and wit' all kinds of etched in designs. But de anchor tis not very purtty and smooth, and like ye say about dis one, dae is funny looking. De anchor goes way down to de very bottom. It ain't seen. Yet, if ye be tied to it, ye knows fer a fact, tis there. Ye has to go mighty deep, sometimes in dashin' billows of deep water to see it. Tis not tall and big like de pillar. Tis moe like a rock, solid and firm. Iffen ye be 'tached to it strongly enough, ye be safe."

Taking the child's hand, Moses led her over to a stool that was old and worn but still sturdy enough to hold his body weight. Sitting down, he picked up the little girl that was the joy of his old age and put her on his knee. "Baby, dey is somethin' stronger dats causing dem pillars to stand firm. Dat be an Anchor. And dat Anchor be Jesus. For iffen He spoke de word and moved de earth beneath, dem pillars wouldn't stand. Cause'n ye find in de Holy Bible where He say, "'I bear up de pillars.'"

"You mean like the song Mammy Zip sings, "Rock of Ages, cleft for me. Let me hide myself in Thee?"

"Yes, Lennie Sarah, 'xactly like de song. Dat Rock of Ages is de secure Anchor.

Chapter 1

Dashing waves of the Ouachita River sloshed against the hull of the mighty Onyx. Tempestuous waters created by the steamer and the upcoming storm did not deter the large vessel as it moved slowly upstream carrying passengers and cargo. Deck hands moved about doing their normal tasks, paying no heed to the storm that threatened to interrupt their mundane duties.

Passengers on the second deck were of diverse backgrounds, from the rich and elite headed to Shreveport to indulge their elaborate lifestyles, to the poor and unfortunate farmers whose land had been confiscated due to delinquent taxes and unpaid debts, and to whom the loan holder refused to extend credit.

One lone passenger, hidden among the boilers, engines, and cargo of the main deck, was anxious about the approaching storm. Daringly, he sneaked between barrels, crates, and stacks of heavy paper wrapped items. Easing to the edge of the deck, he took a worried stare at the dark clouds hovering close, almost seeming to touch the stack at the very top of the Pilot House. He glanced about, but all deck hands were occupied and made no sign of awareness that a stranger was in their midst. The young, unidentified passenger slowly and nonchalantly made his way to the bow of the ship. His eyes traveled up a familiar stately, round object to the point of attraction. Struck by a feeling of awe, he stood fascinated with wonder at the Stars and Stripes flapping ferociously as the wind ripped at its edges and forced the flag from one side of the mast to the other. The stowaway knew all too well, even at his young age, that what the great flag represented was far from true as bitterness and resentment continued to plague some of the states that help make up the nation that he loved. It had been seven years since the end of the devastating Civil War that had split the nation, but its aftermath of hate and division remained.

Although some of the edges were frayed from being whipped about by the fierce wind, the stowaway was still mesmerized at the grandiosity of the Stars and Stripes that had remained firmly secured to the stately mast to which it was attached. "It is attached to an anchor," the young man whispered. "Something solid and stable is holding it." Standing momentarily in silence and reverence, he wiped tears from his eyes with the back of his hand, never removing his gaze from the flag. "Oh, America, America," he uttered. "If only you would stop this bickering and fighting and killing. If only you would unite, how mighty you could be. You must unite to be able to survive the future when other nations come against you with fierce and destroying armies. For *unity* is the anchor that holds a nation together."

The young passenger was unaware that someone had discovered his presence on board until hearing a voice behind him. "Young man, you should get back up to the boiler deck and safe into your cabin. There is a storm brewing."

The stowaway quickly dismissed the fear that threatened to overtake him. Pushing aside the dread that he had been caught and he and his important mission would disappear together from the face of the earth, slowly and without intimidation, he turned and stared into the face of a deck hand. The worker held his stare briefly, before turning and walking away. The stowaway, with an unflinching gaze, was surprised when the deck hand turned around and gave him a big smile.

A blast and loud boom erupted startling both the deck hand and the stowaway. The deck hand took off at a fast run as smoke from the burning Onyx billowed upward.

"The boiler exploded!" A shout rang out as another deck hand came into view. Soon the deck was filled with workers and panicky passengers. Men were yelling. Women were crying. Children were screaming.

"Another steamer has been sabotaged, and no doubt I am to blame," the stowaway whispered. Slipping a hand inside his jacket, he felt the slight bulge beneath his shirt. "You are still safe. I hope we both can survive an explosion and a stormy river."

He looked at the tumultuous waves now covered with smog from a thick, black smoke that overpowered everything within sight. Hesitating only briefly, he put his right hand back inside his jacket and held tightly to a leather pouch about the size of a lady's small purse. He took a deep breath then abandoned ship giving no thought to the raging water below.

Floundering around in the icy waters of the Ouachita River, he was unable to control his movements. He struggled against the turbulent water that lashed about and over him trying to take him under, determined to satisfy its wrath with the flesh and bones of a helpless victim. Exhausted and realizing he was no match for the deadly enemy, he surrendered to the force against him. Exerting every bit of strength he had left, the young man struggled to keep his head above the dashing waves. Surrendering to the current, he drifted far from what once was a secure steamer but now only a heap of burned debris and splinters.

In a very disoriented state, the young man whispered, "Wonder if anyone else survived. Wonder if the deck hand who smiled at me still lives." Having no idea how long or how far he had drifted downstream, he was coherent enough to know he bobbed up and down, occasionally surfacing long enough to breathe deeply before being forced back under to a watery grave. Realizing he was in an eddy, and knowing its current was pulling him downward, he held his breath. Down, down, down, going deeper and deeper into the depth of his captor, he knew it was useless to fight against the eddy. Eventually, his feet would touch bottom, and the eddying current would push him upward and would soon play itself out.

If only there was something I could touch. I reach out but only grasp emptiness and despair. If only there was a mainstay in this seemingly bottomless, watery death trap. This endless floating and drifting with nothing solid to hold onto is stealing every bit of will I have to live and forcing me..... He felt something hard and unyielding against his leg. Feeling himself drifting from the object, he pressed against the force of the undertow. With as much exertion as he could muster up, he drifted back down to the object while endeavoring to shift his body and touch the unmovable hardness with his hand. He managed a couple of quick swipes. *I must breathe. I must breathe. I must get my head above the surface. If my lungs fill up with water that will be the end of me and my mission.*

Allowing the eddy to have its way and letting it push him upward, the young man had no sense of time and direction. When at last he broke through the surface, he was barely coherent enough to keep his face upward as his head bobbled above water. His breathing was slow and shallow. Before surrendering to the overpowering force of his watery enemy, he reflected on the solid object at the bottom of the river. He managed to whisper, "It is. It really is. It's an anchor."

A mighty wave swept over him taking him farther downstream. He felt the waves of slumber lulling him to sleep and angry billows pulling him into the deep. His last thoughts, before yielding to unconsciousness, were of home. *It's like Bethel. Bethel is a safe place, a secure place. Bethel is an anchor.*

Chapter 2

When Nathaniel Hebron and Olaf left the bank of the Boeuf River bordering Bethel Plantation, it was a cold but sunny day in February 1872. With nothing going on at Bethel, it seemed a good day to take out the boat and catch enough fish for Zipporah to cook up a big fish supper. Engrossed in fishing and enjoying a day on the river, the two men were oblivious that the clear sky of the early morning was now covered with dark and threatening clouds until a strong blowing rain beat against the boat.

Carried by blustering waves, the fishing boat drifted downstream with bow and stern tossing up and down like a seesaw. The two anglers offered little resistance knowing they were no rival for the strong wind and torrential rain that threatened to capsize their wooden vessel. Although a bit oversized and sturdily built, it was no match against the vehement, destructive force raging across the Boeuf River in Northeast Louisiana.

The fierce wind tore at their already none too sturdy overhead covering. While affording some shelter, it could not compare to the damaging, cyclonic squall that was ripping and threatening to tear it to pieces and leave parts scattered here and there, decorating the Boeuf and Ouachita Rivers. Using long paddles, Nate and Olaf did their best to guide the boat westward. In the distance they spotted a place where land jutted out into the river.

"We are at the mouth of the Ouachita where Boeuf River flows into Black Lake!" Nate said, yelling to be heard above the dashing waves and the noise of their flimsy canopy flapping in the wind. "Let's try and get a little closer to land before we drop anchor!"

"Over there, Mr. Nate, lets drop anchor near that headland!" Olaf shouted. "Maybe we can secure everythin' and go ashore before we drown in dis gully washer!"

"Okay, but we can't get too close to the bank. The strong wind will slam the boat into it and rip the hull! We best stop here!"

Dropping anchor, they endeavored to fasten down their fishing gear. The boat continued to drift in a semi-circle on the turbulence, but it stayed secured to the anchor as if in defiance of the unwelcome intruder that interrupted the planned relaxing fishing day of the two men.

"Ye think we can swim to shore and find some kind o' shelter from de storm?" Olaf asked. "If we stay in dis boat and it fills up wit' water, we gonna join dat anchor at de bottom of de Boeuf River."

Nate lifted the top of what served as a seat at the stern of the boat. He removed a large black plastic bag and a small first aid kit then handed them to Olaf. "We may not have to swim." Removing his shoes, rolling up the legs of his pants and easing out of the boat as it continued to drift one way and then the other, Nate held onto the side and lowered himself into the water. He went deeper and deeper as Olaf stared in wonder.

"Mr. Nate, what ye doing? Ye trying to drown yoself? Miz Leah will have my hide if somethin' happens to ye! Git back in dis boat!"

Still holding on to the side of the fishing boat with water covering his shoulders, Nate replied, "I am standing on the bottom, Olaf. We don't have to swim ashore. We can walk."

Nate held the black bag firmly, as Olaf removed his shoes, rolled up the legs of his pants and joined him in the water. With arms up, the two men pressed against the wind and waves while managing to keep a grip on the bag. At the sound of a loud boom, they stood petrified in knee deep water.

"What was that, Mr. Nate?"

Seeing billowing smoke rising higher and higher, Nate replied, "Something exploded. Come on, let's get to land."

By the time they reached the shore of the headland, they were in only two feet of water but had trudged through mud and slime that clung to their feet and legs. Making their way to a cluster of small trees not far from shore, the men scraped up some limbs and weeds, took matches from the first aid kit and endeavored to get a fire going.

"We may have more smoke than flame but maybe it will help take the chill away," Nate said as the men snuggled up in two small blankets that Olaf had taken from the plastic bag.

After the storm finally passed and the sun was peeking its way between breaks in the clouds, the two men waded back through mud and water and climbed into their boat. Fortunately for them, it had survived and was still afloat, attached to the anchor.

After returning the black bag and first aid kit to the storage at the rear of the vessel, Olaf took out the binoculars. Looking out over the water, his eyes came to rest on something downstream a distance from where they were anchored. "Mr. Nate, I see somethin' floatin' over there. Ye better take a look."

Nate looked in the direction he was pointing. "I believe there is something." Taking the binoculars, he brought into focus what Olaf had spotted. "I don't think it is just something. I am pretty sure it's somebody."

"If it be, whoever it be, is daed. No doubt drowned during dat storm."

"Pull up anchor and let's check it out."

Olaf pulled on the anchor rope. "It won't break loose, Mr. Nate! The anchor is too secure!"

Instead of helping with the anchor, Nate hurriedly took off his jacket and jumped into the river hitting the cold water with a big splash before Olaf could say another word. He looked on wide eyed.

"No, Mr. Nate, come back! Ye might drown yoself! The water is still rough and dangerous!"

Nate was already swimming away. He called back. "Stay attached to the anchor but head this way. Get as close as you can then throw out the lifeline." Nate allowed the current to carry him downstream, but it was, also, to his disadvantage as it carried the victim away from him. Seemingly, the two were drifting farther apart as the waves beat against them both. He saw the victim go under water then rise again, his head bobbling up and down. He knew for sure then, it was not something but someone. *It's a young man. He's flailing his arms. He is going to drown himself.*

"Quit fighting! Relax and float! You are going to drown yourself! I'm coming to you!" Nate stopped shouting and focused on swimming toward his goal. *Jesus, please keep him alive. Don't let him die. I am almost to him. Don't let him die within my reach.*

Being young and a good swimmer and with the help of the current, Nate covered the watery path getting closer and closer to the victim. *Oh, it can't be. My brain must be waterlogged. He is supposed to be in Washington.* Nate released all the energy he could muster up to swim faster. *It is him. But what is he doing this close to Bethel?* Finally within reach, he moved a little closer and approached the victim from behind. Putting an arm around his chest, Nate held the man's head above water, dragging him while kicking himself back toward the boat.

He glanced over his shoulder. Olaf was moving toward them. "It's Malachi! Throw out the lifeline!" Nate continued to swim backward, dragging Malachi along while Olaf hurriedly took the lifeline and threw it toward the two men.

"I've got it! I've got it! Pull us in!" Barely above a whisper, he said, "Hold on Malachi. We will be at Bethel soon."

As Olaf drew the line in toward the boat, Nate struggled to hold onto Malachi while clutching tightly to the lifeline. "He is still breathing. Oh Jesus, don't let him die. We are really anchored to You. For no man can save another unless You will it. Oh, please, don't let my brother die."

Chapter 3

With a pillow cushioning his back, Malachi leaned against the headboard of his bed and recalled the past two days. After Nate and Olaf recused him from the river and made it to Bethel, he had enjoyed and relished the attention of Momma and Dove. Zip had hovered over him like a mother hen over her little chicks.

Memories of his childhood and maturing into a young man at Bethel Plantation filled his mind. *It is so good to be home at Bethel. Bethel is a safe place. Even if something should happen and destroy Bethel House, I will be safe because Papa and Momma and the rest of my family will still be here. They are the anchor that makes Bethel a secure stronghold.*

"However, as much as I like coddling, enough is enough," he murmured. "I am so tired of this idleness." Throwing back the warm covers, he sat up on the side of the bed as thoughts continued to bombard him. *Not having to constantly be aware of my surroundings and looking over my shoulder for fear of being attacked has settled my mind and nerves, but I must leave. I have a job to do.* A sound interrupted his thoughts. He sat very still and listened as Zipporah's voice filled the house.

"Well, sometimes out on life's ocean.
I begin to feel like I's all alone.
O's, but I's not discouraged by the raging billows.
I's can make it, O, yesss.., I's shorely can make it.
Cause I's got Jesus. He's de Anchor.
Hmm... He's de Anchor o' my soul."

"Wow! Nobody can do it like Zip. I really have missed her singing. There is one thing for sure, however, if I wait for the females in this house to give me permission to get out of this bed, I will be stuck here until Thanksgiving and Christmas. That can't be."

Sitting on the bed a while longer and meditating, he recognized a familiar odor wafting its way up the stairs. Taking a deep breath and savoring the moment, a smell from his childhood engulfed him. "Hmm, Zip's fried bacon and flapjacks."

Quietly, he opened the bedroom door and looked both directions down the hall. "The coast is clear," he whispered. Grinning and tiptoeing out of his room, cautiously he went down the stairs. Hearing voices coming from the sitting room, he paused near the door and listened. A smile creased his face at the sound of his mother's voice.

"Samuel, he is our son. We have a right to know what he was doing at the mouth of the Boeuf and Ouachita Rivers. It was the mercy of Jesus that Nathaniel and Olaf went fishing in this cold February weather and saved him from drowning or freezing to death."

"Yes, Mother," Samuel replied.

"He may be in some kind of trouble."

"Yes, Mother."

"He is supposed to be in Washington doing some kind of government work. Sometimes he works very closely to the President." Tabitha paused in thought. She gave Samuel a look filled with concern and fear. "Oh, my! Do you think the President could have sent him on a secret assignment? If so, his life may be in danger."

"Yes, Mother."

"Did you look inside the leather pouch that Nathaniel found floating on top of the water not far from where he rescued Malachi?"

"Yes, Mother."

"Did you read the contents of the water proof envelope?"

"No, Mother."

"Samuel Hebron, you are exasperating."

Silence prevailed. Malachi moved closer to the door barely able to squelch a chuckle when he heard Papa's reply.

"And you, Tabitha Hebron, are beautiful. A bit nosey into your grown son's affairs but still the most beautiful woman in the world. If Malachi is on a secret assignment…"

Thinking he better move before Momma discovered he was out of bed, Malachi tiptoed across the parlor and into the kitchen. Zip was at the stove concentrating on the sizzling bacon. Her melodious voice had changed from singing to humming and she was paying no attention to what was going on in the rest of Bethel House. Sneaking up on her backside, he poked her ribs and said, "Boo."

"Ooh….weee!" Zip squealed and shuttered, her whole body shaking.

Malachi roared with laughter and reached to the plate of bacon resting beside the stove, snatching two pieces quickly before Zip could gain her composure.

"Malachi Hebron, ye gonna be de death of poe ole Zip. Ye bout made me jump outa my skin." She swatted him lightly with the dish cloth she was clutching.

"Aw, Zip, when you jump out, I'd jump in, but it would take all of the Hebron family to fill your skin."

"Boy, ye better watch yo tongue and quit dat stealing bacon. Ye wait til de family sits down to de breakfast table like a civilized young'un should. One of des days, I's gonna beat dat meanness outa ye."

Wrapping both arms around her, Malachi leaned his head against her back. "I sure do love you, Zip."

Zip stopped her cooking, turned and enfolded him in her arms, almost smothering him in an embrace. "Os Mr. Malachi, Zip sho is glad ye be home. I wuz so skeered when Mr. Nate and Olaf brung ye to de house dat ye wuz gonna die fer sho. I sho do love ye." Zip released him. "Now, ye git yoself up dem stairs and git some clothes on. Ye ain't gonna come to my table in jammies. Miz Tabitha will have a conniption fit." She swatted his back side with a spatula when he turned to leave. "Now, git!"

"Yes mam. Cook those flapjacks extra brown just for me, Zip," he said with a grin.

Entering the parlor he saw Samuel and Tabitha standing in the doorway of the sitting room with looks of astonishment. "Malachi!" They said in unison.

"Morning, Papa. Morning, Momma." Still grinning, he headed up the stairs. Stepping into the upstairs hall, he almost lost his balance when a little nine year old streak with long blonde hair hanging loosely down her back slammed into him. Throwing both arms around his waist and squeezing him as tightly as her little arms could, she said, "Oh Malachi. You are out of bed. You are well. I love you."

Malachi picked the little girl up holding to her waist tightly and swinging her around as Dove squealed with delight. Putting her back on her feet, he laughed as she staggered with dizziness and her merriment drifted all over Bethel House. "Dove Hebron, I love you, too." He took her hand. "Wait for me in my room and we will go downstairs together."

"But…but you are not dressed."

"I will dress in the bathroom." While getting dressed, Malachi's thoughts went back to a little five year old girl. He and Sarah had found her in their search for Levi after the stagecoach they were on wrecked. She was huddled against the wheel of the coach, crying and shaking with fear.

Returning to his room, the little girl was sitting on his bed patiently waiting. He took her hand. "I am so glad you are a Hebron. That you are one of us, Dove. Sarah married Levi and doesn't live at

Bethel anymore because they have their own house at Blossom Hill. With Anna away and my job keeping me so busy, you are such a comfort to Papa and Momma."

Dove looked up at him. "Thanks, Malachi, for saving me. My other Papa and Momma were killed, and I was left so alone. I felt lost and helpless. You and Sarah took care of me and brought me here. Now I live at Bethel House and haven't been lost or alone since I've come here. I feel safe and secure at Bethel with Papa and Momma and Zip." She removed her hand from his and wrapped both arms around his waist.

Malachi squeezed her tightly then took her hand, again. "Now, how about we get downstairs and join Papa and Momma for breakfast and fill up on Zip's bacon and flapjacks."

Chapter 4

Malachi awoke with a start. Not sure what had disturbed his much needed sleep, he turned over and stared at the ceiling. All seemed well. With heavy eyelids, he mumbled, "Sleep. Wonderful sleep." An unusual noise shook him back to full consciousness. He bolted upright then slung his legs over the side of the bed. He listened. *Sounds like shuffling of feet just outside my door. Someone is there.* His eyes were glued on the door. *There is no mistake about it. That door knob is moving.* He watched. The movement stopped. He waited. The silence was creepy. *It is not the maid. She would knock then use her key.* When the knob moved again and the noise was louder, he stood to his feet keeping his eyes on the door. He heard someone whispering. Then all was quiet.

Tiptoeing over to the window of the room at the boarding house where he had stopped for the night and pushing aside the curtain, he whispered, "It's dark out there. No one should be stirring this time of night." He turned at the loud rattling of the door knob. "Someone is stirring, and whoever it is wants in my room." Making his way in the dark, he felt around on the bed for his clothes. He dared not turn on the gas lantern for fear that whoever was lurking and trying to get into the room would see the light and wait for him by the door. After getting dressed, he removed the leather pouch from its hiding place beneath the bed covers and dropped it inside his shirt. Removing his duffle bag from beneath the bed, he picked it up and tiptoed back over to the window. *You might know, it's stuck. Just my luck.* However, with some exertion of energy, the window broke loose, squeaking as it yielded to the pressure. Malachi managed to raise the glass as far up as it would go. The small window was too high from the floor for him to crawl through. He stood in the darkness, pondering his next move.

Hmm. I have to act fast. I need something to stand on to be able to grip the sides of the window, then I can squeeze my way through the opening. Feeling his way, he tiptoed over to a small crude desk, the only piece of furniture in the room other than the bed. The drawer of the desk was loose and easily slipped out. Turning it upside down under the window, he grabbed his bag and was about to toss it out the opening when he remembered the pistol. Stepping off the drawer and hurrying to the bed, he threw back the sheet and picked up the small weapon. Placing it in the inside pocket of his jacket, he hastened back to the window. After tossing the duffle bag outside, he forced himself through the small opening. With a thud, his body hit the hard unyielding earth. Picking up his bag and not bothering to brush the dirt from his clothes, he hesitated only long enough to be sure the leather pouch was secure then rushed away from the building. Dashing quickly behind a bush not far from the boarding house, he peeked around the edge just in time to see a shadow appear at the window where he had just escaped. A voice drifted through the opening.

"The little traitor. He's escaped us again."

"Don't worry, we'll get him this time. He's headed to Texas. Come on, let's get to the train depot."

Two distinct voices. So, my pursuer has an accomplice. Malachi sneaked up to the corner of the building. The dim light of the lamp post cast forth enough brightness so he could see two men as they rushed out the door of the boarding house and headed lickety spit in the direction of the depot.

"They expect me to hop the train." He snickered. Being cautious even in the dark, he made his way to the town road. There were a few lamp posts scattered around Shreveport's busy hub. To avoid being seen, he stayed in the darkness and headed to the livery. Walking past horse stalls and making his way to the back of the stables, he knocked on a shabby wooden door, faded and streaked from use over the years. Not receiving a response, he knocked a little louder. Still not hearing a noise, he called, "Hosea. Hosea, let me in." He waited anxiously while staying alert knowing he could be attacked at any moment. Hearing a sound come from inside the room, he breathed a sigh of relief knowing Hosea had gotten out of bed and was headed to the door.

"Who's there?"

"Open up, Hosea. It's Malachi. Let me in. Hurry."

Hosea removed the latch from the door. "Malachi, what is it? What's your hurry?"

Malachi rushed into the room. "Flip the latch, quickly."

Hosea did as he was told. "What you doing getting an old man out of bed this time of the morning. Precious is the little sleep I do get, and when I finally do, I get woke up by a young man who is wandering around all hours of the night. It's not even daylight, yet. Do you ever sleep?"

"Not much, Hosea. I'm sorry, but I needed to hide out some place for a couple of hours."

"Oh, okay, boy. You in some kind of trouble? What kind of secrets you got hidden away this time?

"I am on government business."

"Yeah, I figured it was government business. What kind of government business?"

"I can't tell you that. It would put you in too much danger."

Hosea walked to a small table and was about to turn on a gas lantern but halted at Malachi's voice.

"No, don't turn on a light. You go on back to bed. My pursuers headed to the train depot, but when they discover I am not there, they no doubt will scour the town looking for me. It is possible, but not likely, they may go ahead and board the train thinking I hid out in the baggage car and can nab me later down the tracks."

"You want me to tie a horse around back for you just in case you have to leave in a hurry?"

"I'll do it. I wanted to let you know what I was doing so you wouldn't mistake me for a horse thief. I won't be long. Latch this door and let me in through the back entrance."

Hosea walked to the back of his small living quarters and waited. Soon he heard a tap on the door and Malachi joined him inside. "Maybe I better not tarry. I don't want to be the cause of something bad happening to you."

"Oh, don't you worry about me. Hosea can take care of himself. I'm stronger than I...."

There was a loud rap on the door. The men exchanged looks. "You better skedaddle, Malachi."

"I'm out of here. Don't let them know you saw me. Thanks, Hosea."

Two more loud raps sounded on the door before Hosea ambled to it. "What you want?" He grumbled.

"Open up!"

"I am not gonna open up until I know who's at my door."

"I said open up. You better do it if you know what's good for you."

"I know what is not good for me. That is for an old man to be woke up in the middle of the night by hoodlums, or whoever you are, and expect me to open my door. Get away from here."

"If you don't open it, I am going to knock it down!"

Hosea hesitated. *Malachi should be a good distance from here by now.* "Okay, just a minute." He opened the door, mumbling under his breath the whole time.

"Quit mumbling old man and turn on some light."

"What do you want from me this time of the night. If it's a horse you want, we can do that at daylight in the livery." Fumbling around on the lamp table with his hand, Hosea knocked a book off to the floor. The loud noise as it hit the wooden surface gave him the opportunity he needed. Taking advantage of the moment, he opened the drawer of the small table and took out his gun. Stalling for time, he continued to fumble around on the table. The intruder was getting very impatient.

"Hurry up. Get that light on! What are you fumbling around for?"

"Trying to find the matches to light the lantern. If you think you can do any better, come do it."

In the darkness, the intruder stumbled around until finding the bed. Keeping a hand on it, he made his way to the lamp table. Bumping into Hosea, he grumbled, "Get out of the way."

Stepping aside and waiting for the right moment, when the intruder turned his back Hosea whacked him across the back of the head with the butt of his gun. Reaching to the lantern, he turned a knob and the light came on. Hosea grinned. "The bluff worked. You really aren't very smart, but I reckon it don't take a lot of smart to steal and kill." Taking hold of the man's arms, he drug him out of his living quarters into the livery. "Mister, if you have any smart, at least enough to know what is good for you, as soon as you come to your senses, you will get far away from here as fast as you can." He chuckled. "Headache and all."

Returning to his living quarters, Hosea walked to the back door and looked out. A light tint in the eastern sky let him know daybreak was approaching. "Good luck, Malachi. It is the breaking of a new day. Sure hope you accomplish your mission."

Chapter 5

Malachi rode with haste from Shreveport, north along the Louisiana State Line, turned west and entered Texas just above Longview. Crossing a small creek near the mouth of the Sabine River, he had flash backs of when he and Sarah crossed over Sandy Creek in their search for Levi. Not slowing his gait to rest, although it was tempting, he rode fast and hard. The horse hooves caused big splashes in the water and buried a little deeper the rocks that formed the bed of the clear stream. He would have relished a few relaxing moments but dared not take the risk. His pursuer or pursuers were dogging his trail and most likely were only a short distance behind him.

Galloping across East Texas, frequently he took detours forming a maze hoping to mislead and distract whoever was trailing him. Knowing he was on a dangerous mission, his thoughts turned to his brother Gideon and his brother-in-law, Benjamin Drestan. They worked together to get him a job with the government, although under protest from them both. He had insisted. Gideon tried to made him promise not to take any dangerous assignments, but he had refused to commit. Admitting to himself, on some occasions he wondered if he had answered too hastily. This was one of those times and a feeling of trepidation nudged at his mind as he recalled his reply to his brother's protest. *But I like excitement. I don't mind taking a risk. If it happens to be a little dangerous, well, so be it.*

Automatically responding to a prickling of dread, Malachi touched the pistol in his pocket. Feeling it gave him a small reprieve from his anxiety. Putting a hand inside his shirt and resting it against the leather pouch, he released a sigh of relief. "I still have you. Sure do hope until this mission is accomplished, you and the important information will remain with me. However, there are a few more places to go and things to do, so it will still be a while before we can head to Washington D.C."

Recalling Gideon's continued protest, an alarm went off in his brain. *What you are doing goes beyond risk and challenge, Malachi. It is more than a little dangerous. One minute you may be alive and the next minute dead.*

At the moment, his reply seemed very futile. *But Gid, you and Benjamin have undertaken dangerous assignments and survived. Benjamin, you were a spy during the war. Wasn't that a dangerous risk? And when you and Hannah went to rescue Nate from a prisoner of war camp, you both were in a very precarious situation. You dressing and acting the part of a Union Officer and Hannah posing as your nurse.*

With set mind and determination, he rode through unfamiliar territory trying to push aside the fact that maybe he was too hasty and eager in justifying his actions. *Gid, not only were you in danger as a major in the war, but also afterwards when you entered a hideout on Brewster Estate and faced down the train robber and Brewster, the instigator and a number one outlaw. You took the dangerous risk that they would be captured before they could kill you. In your search for Abigail, you took many risks, but you felt she was worth it and didn't stop until you found her, and until the thieves and her abductor met their fate.*

Malachi, that's different. I am the oldest son. You are the youngest. Just think of what it would do to Papa and Momma if something happened to you.

Hold on, Gid. It is not different. You mean as much to Papa and Momma as I do. This is something I want to do, and nothing is going to happen to me.

Malachi smiled, remembering the look on Gid's face as he replied. It was a look that portrayed uncertainty but also of respect and pride. *There is no way you can know that it won't. Yet, you seem to have no doubt. How can you be that sure?*

His reply to Gid's question was so vivid in his mind that he spoke it aloud. "Because Gid, I have a Stronghold, an Anchor. The solid and secure Rock of Ages that Zip sings about."

As Malachi rode on knowing danger was lurking behind, in front, and beside him, he could almost hear Zip's melodious voice. Wishing he was standing just outside the kitchen door and listening to her sing, he longed to be at Bethel. "I can't do it like you, Zip," he said, pushing aside his homesickness, "but here it goes."

"Rock of Ages, cleft for me.

Let me hide myself in Thee.

Nothing in my hand I bring.

Simply to Thy cross I cling."

Not caring that his singing could bring his would be attackers upon him, his voice drifted through the clearing of tree branches. Sometimes singing the words and sometimes humming the tune, making melody with the leaves rustling in the soft breeze. He felt assured in the fact that no circumvention or chance would hinder or control the firm resolve of determination to accomplish his mission.

Entering the outskirts of Fort Worth, Texas, Malachi realized the feeling of fear that had tried to shake his confidence was gone. "Yes, Gid," he whispered, "I may get a little shaky and fearful, but I am attached to the Anchor that is steadfast. He keeps me stable. That Anchor is Jesus. As long as I cleave to the Rock of Ages, I am hidden in the cleft of that solid Rock, nothing can happen to me unless He allows it. Therefore, 'I will not be afraid what flesh can do unto me.'"

Resolute and unafraid, he pulled the horse to a stop. He had business with his old friend, Sheriff Obid. Placing the reins around the hitching post in front of a building, he hurried inside. Hesitating near the door and looking around, he called, "Sheriff? Sheriff Obid, are you here?" Not getting a response, he sat down in a chair by the sheriff's desk. Feeling confident with his assignment, he was anxious to know if Sheriff Obid had some information for him. He closed his eyes, and immediately flashbacks from the first time he had come to this office filled his mind. After the stagecoach he and Sarah were on wrecked, they and the driver of the stage, Jabin, had come to Sheriff Obid with a satchel full of money and a little girl whose parents were killed in the accident. She was so sad and alone. He smiled. Today, she is happy as a lark and Bethel is her home. God does take the bad things that happen to us and replaces them with something good.

"Why, Malachi, I didn't expect you until next week."

At the sound of the sheriff's voice, Malachi opened his eyes. Sheriff Obid continued. "I have one name for you. However, you had better check him out. I'm only going on what I picked up here and there. Can't prove anything."

"I am early. Being forced to leave Shreveport in a big hurry when...."

Malachi was interrupted by an abrupt opening of the door and a young man rushing inside. "Sheriff Obid, there is...." He stopped speaking at the sight of Malachi.

"It's okay, deputy. You can speak in front of him. What's the problem?"

"I was at the barber shop waiting my turn and a stranger in town was in the barber's chair. He asked Jesse about some man. Jesse asked what he wanted with the man. The stranger replied, he's got something I want and after I get it I'm probably gonna kill him. Yep, he said, I'm gonna kill him for giving me such a hard chase."

"Did the stranger give the man's name?"

"Yes sir. Malachi Hebron."

"Well, Deputy Dan, meet Malachi Hebron."

The deputy's eyes bulged. "You're...you are Malachi Hebron?"

"That I am."

The young deputy swayed on his feet. Sheriff Obid laid his hand on the young man's arm. "Steady, now."

"He.....he....," Dan stuttered.

"Relax, Dan." Sheriff Obid said. "What are you afraid of? The stranger doesn't know this is Malachi."

"He...he... had a picture. He showed it to Jesse and said this is Malachi Hebron. He said after he got a bite to eat he was coming to the sheriff's office."

"Go to the diner and keep an eye on him."

Deputy Dan opened the door then closed it quickly. "He's coming, Sheriff. He's almost here."

"Get in a cell, Malachi. Hurry," the sheriff said.

Malachi rushed into the cell. The door clicked behind him and Sheriff Obid turned the key. Making sure he still had his pistol and leather pouch, he lay down on the cot with his face to the wall. Taking the pistol out of his shirt and holding it in his hand with his arm close to his side, he pulled a blanket up to his ears.

Chapter 6

The conversation going on outside his cell brought an unexpected snicker of laughter from Malachi. Quickly covering the noise with a fake snore, he lay very still pushing aside the urge to turn over and sneak a peek at his pursuer.

"Lock him up, Dan!" Sheriff Obid demanded.

"What do you mean, lock me up?" The stranger grumbled. "All I did was walk in here and ask about a man I have business with."

"What kind of business?"

"That's personal! I don't have to answer that question!"

Sheriff Obid pointed a finger in the man's face. "When you come into this office, you are required to answer any question I ask if I want you to. And I want you to. Lock him up, Dan."

Dan took hold of the man's arm but dropped it when the stranger gave him a hard slap across the wrist. "On what grounds?"

"I have it on good authority that you are looking for a man and have plans for his demise when you find him. What better reason than murder do I need."

"That's right," the man shouted as Dan gave his arm a firm grip. "He's got something I want, and I plan to get it one way or another."

"You will not do it in my town. Put him in the other cell, Dan. Uh… give him some coffee." The sheriff pulled out the small drawer of his desk. He took out a piece of paper and a small packet. Walking to where Dan was preparing the coffee for the prisoner, he laid the packet beside the cup. "Add this to the coffee," he whispered.

Malachi lay very still with lips pressed tightly together, afraid to move, lest he be unable to squelch the chuckle that was desperately trying to push its way up through his throat and out his mouth.

Several minutes passed before he felt the hand of Sheriff Obid on his shoulder.

"Get up, Malachi. The man is asleep. Hurry but be quiet. You have to get away from here."

Malachi sat up on the side of the cot. Putting the pistol inside his shirt and under his belt, he stood to his feet. "Thanks Sheriff Obid. I have gathered some important information that I must get to D.C. That is, after I make a few more stops."

Sheriff Obid handed Malachi the slip of paper he had removed from the desk drawer. "Here is the name of the man I was talking about."

Malachi put the paper inside the leather pouch, tiptoed out of the cell, cast a quick glance at the prisoner and walked to the door of the sheriff's office.

The sheriff followed him outside. "If you want to take the train to Austin, you'll be okay. This guy is going to be here for a few hours. Dan put some sleeping powder in his coffee."

⚓⚓⚓

With exuberance and anticipation, Malachi hurried through the gate and up the walk that graced the grounds of the imperial building. Having been here before, he was familiar with the dozen steps spanning the entire length of the front entrance. Usually, he was somewhat amazed as to why anyone would think it worthwhile to put so much time and expense into such a waste, but today, his mind was on something more important. Preoccupied with his mission, he didn't even notice the many thousands of Austin brick that covered the exterior of the impressive structure. The ornamental designs at the top and base of the six fluted ionic columns that lined the façade did not distract him.

Malachi walked through the double doors of the governor's mansion in Austin, Texas, into an elaborate entry way with marble floors and exquisite columns that spanned the full height of the entrance hall of the three story building. The mosaic ceiling with golden chandeliers spoke of wealth but was cold and uninviting. *Sure am glad I don't have to live here. It speaks of unrest and danger. Makes me even more thankful for the peace and safety of Bethel.*

Walking over to a counter located in the entry way, he put his travel bag to the side. Several security guards were ambling about, but none seemed to be interested in him. When Malachi walked down the entry hall, his shoes making a clopping noise as they hit the marble floors, the guards snapped to attention. He paused in front of a painting hanging on the wall above a Queen Anne davenport. He had seen it many times, but it always intrigued him. The words at the bottom of the painting arrested the attention of all visitors to the mansion. "Remember the Alamo," he whispered.
Although not a Texan, he felt great respect for the men who had given their lives to defend what rightly belonged to them.

Absorbed in the painting, his mind went back to a more recent war. *I was too young to be active in the war, but Papa, Gid, and Nate were in the heat of battle more than once. And Hannah risked her life as a successful Confederate Spy.* Malachi knew were it not for the amazing grace and mercy of Jesus, a painting of them as casualties of the cruel war that swept through the south like a vicious tornado could be hanging on a wall in some building. He remembered how Sarah, at only sixteen years old, faced down a northern renegade and shot him to protect Anna, Fancy and herself. Wiping away tears of thankfulness, he recalled how Momma, Hannah and others had taken in wounded soldiers, turning Bethel House into a hospital and nursing back to health those who would have died otherwise. He spoke aloud with grave admiration. "Bethel became a stronghold for them and gave them a glimmer of hope. Something they could cling to and hold onto until they were able to travel. Bethel was like an anchor for the wounded, the sick, and the fearful."

He stood in silence and solemnity. So engrossed in his thoughts and the painting, he was unaware someone had walked up and stood slightly behind him until a quiet voice asked, "You okay, Malachi?"

Malachi turned. "Oh, officer, I'm sorry. This painting always captivates me."

"Yes. I can see that it has an effect on you. The Governor is expecting you."

Malachi followed the man up a flight of stairs and waited while the officer tapped lightly on a door before barely opening it. "Governor, Malachi Hebron is here."

At the governor's bidding, Malachi followed the officer into the room. The Governor of Texas stood to his feet. "Wait outside, Officer Casey. Sit down, Malachi."

Chapter 7

Malachi removed the leather pouch from inside his shirt, unzipped it and took out two pieces of paper. He handed them to Governor Davis and sat at attention while the Governor unfolded the larger one. As the Governor read the list, Malachi watched his countenance go from mere curiosity, to worried, then to disbelief.

Without even a glance at the young man sitting at his desk, Governor Davis put the list aside and picked up the other slip of paper. After opening up the single fold, his incredulous look would have caused any observer to doubt the validity of the information it revealed. Leaning forward in his chair, the Governor looked at Malachi with an expression of debatable horror. Staring with mouth agape, he seemed unable to speak.

Malachi waited. His eyes were fastened on the man who had the respect of not only his own staff but that of high ranking government officials, including the President of the United States.

"Incredible," the Governor uttered. "Are….are you sure about this, Malachi?"

"Well, as of now, no sir. Sheriff Obid said there is no positive evidence but enough suspicion to definitely check him out."

"I know Obid. He would not have given you the name unless he was pretty sure the accusations could be proven." The Governor paused. "But…this man is one of my top aides." Pushing his chair away from the desk, in silence he walked to the window of his office and gazed out at the skyline of the capital city of the state he governed.

Malachi waited while the seconds ticked by. Knowing he needed to be on the road, anxiousness almost overcame him. It took all his self-control to sit still.

The Governor turned, walked back to his desk, leaned forward pounding on his chest and spoke rather loudly, "I have trusted this man with my own life!"

Malachi observed the stern and determined look on his face. Having been with Governor Davis on several occasions, he had never known the Governor to raise his voice in mirth or anger. He stared goggle eyed at the man before him, not sure if he even dared to breathe.

The Governor stood up straight. Holding the slip of paper in his hand, he shook it at Malachi. "Yet, this is accusing him of being involved in a most serious crime." Picking up the other list, he continued. "This is serious business. Those on this list can be sent to prison, but this." He shook the slip of paper at Malachi, again. "This goes beyond mere seriousness. If found guilty, he will be hanged." He hung his head and whispered, "Yes, I have trusted this man with my life on several occasions. He could have taken me out at any given moment."

"I....I'm sorry, Governor," Malachi stuttered.

"Why should you be sorry? You are just doing your job."

"Yes sir," Malachi said, wiping his brow. "But I must have your permission to have him investigated. You can stop it before it gets started."

"Have him investigated. Justice says a man is innocent until proven guilty. I must admit, justice doesn't rule in this day, sad to say. It seems as if the rule today is guilty until proven innocent. And proven innocent doesn't seem to take priority. Some folks had rather believe good is bad and bad is good. What a warped sense of justice." The Governor paused, walked over and stood in front of Malachi.

"Do your job, Malachi. If this man is proven innocent, he has nothing to worry about. But until then, if he is guilty, your life is also in danger. He and his accomplices will stop at nothing to prevent you from getting this information to Washington." Handing both pieces of paper to Malachi, the Governor waited while he put them back into the leather pouch, zipped it closed and dropped it down his shirt.

Malachi stood. "Thank you, Governor Davis."

The Governor shook his hand. "You be careful. You are a young man with many years to live, God permitting. Be sure you stay alive to live each day to the fullest."

Making his way down the stairs, Malachi walked toward the area where he had left his travel bag. It was no longer there. Approaching the counter, he looked all around, but the bag was nowhere to be seen. "Hmm," he uttered, a bit perplexed. Walking slowly about the entrance hall, looking behind chairs, in corners, and under the davenport which he was about to slide away from the wall, his search was interrupted when Officer Casey approached him.

"Lost something, Malachi? A guard came upstairs and told me you are snooping around down here."

Malachi looked at the man. "No, I didn't lose anything. I know precisely where I left it. Someone has moved or stolen my travel bag." He chuckled. "I can't imagine what anyone would want with that jumbled up mess. Dirty clothes and clean clothes all mixed together and a present for my girl."

Officer Casey replied, "Well, let's take a look outside."

The men looked around the grounds of the Governor's mansion but found nothing. After giving his thanks and farewell to the officer, Malachi hastened down the main street in the city of Austin, Texas. He put his hand over his chest feeling the leather pouch hidden beneath his shirt. *I know what whoever stole my travel bag was looking for but didn't dare tell Officer Casey. Just wish I knew who he is. Whoever he is knows me, where I am, and what's inside this little pouch. It's going to take somebody smarter than him to thwart my mission.*

Carefully surveying the area as he made his way to the train depot a rundown building caught his eye. After studying the outside awhile, he walked across the yard and up three squeaky steps. The door creaked as he pushed it open just enough to ease his slim body through. Hesitating to be sure the creaking didn't cause a reaction from within, he slipped through the opening. It didn't take him long to realize he was an intruder into a domain that had already been claimed. Much to his chagrin, he was greeted heartily and quickly, entangled in the film of a sticky, silky spider web.

"Will you walk into my parlor said a spider to a fly. Tis the prettiest little parlor that ever you did spy." He couldn't help but grin while quoting the poem that Momma had read to him so many times. She often reminded him of it when she felt he may be lured into something that looked harmless but was really a web of deceit. The grin on his face disappeared as his eyes roved around the large entrance room. *Was I just lured into a web of deceit and danger?* Looking at a curved and unkept staircase, the next two lines of the simple poem came to him. "The way into my parlor is up a winding stair. And I have many pretty things to show when you are there." Shuddering, he eased a little closer to the staircase. *It's just a poem, Malachi.* He walked to the foot of the stairs. He stopped, alert for any movement or sound. His eyes slowly followed the winding staircase. Nothing. All was still and quiet. Lifting his foot to take the first step, the next lines of the poem hit him with full force. "Oh, no, no! said the little fly, to ask me is in vain, for who goes up your winding stair can ne're come down again."

His foot froze in midair. "That does it. Better not chance it. That silly little poem came to me for a reason." Seeing a back door exit, he stepped outside and stumbled over his travel bag. It was opened and the contents were scattered over the ground. Quickly, he picked up his belongings and stuffed them into the bag. He glanced around for the gift but it was nowhere to be seen. "Oh, well, better get away from here while I can." Taking a precautious look around and upward, he spied a gun pointed at him from an upstairs window. There was no time to think. A bullet went whizzing through the air barely missing him by a thread. Being slim and spry enabled him to move quickly and escape unharmed. In a fast run down the street, he paused for breath long enough to utter, "So long, Mr. Spider, you didn't get me this time."

Chapter 8

Deborah Dotson strolled past the dairy barn then wandered along the path where the milk cows were grazing. Pausing briefly at the fence and looking out across the pasture, childhood memories made their way to the forefront of her brain. She smiled, recalling how she and her brother, Luke, had tried to name all of the cows. After about a dozen names they had given up because so many of the cows were alike, and they couldn't distinguish one from the other. Although she cherished her memories of growing up on the farm located in a beautiful valley near Pueblo, Colorado, they did not help her mood today. Other things crowded her thoughts, troubling her excessively.

She followed a path that weaved its way in and out among the aspen and hawthorne trees with their beautiful spring foliage gracing the surroundings. Relishing the late spring zephyr that lifted strains of her long brunette hair, she removed the loose tresses from her face and walked upon the bridge that spanned the small creek. Half way of the bridge, she paused and looked out across the Wet Mountain range that surrounded the Dotson farm. "I love the mountains," she uttered. "Nothing can compare to the fresh mountain air." Usually a walk around the farm cleared her mind and eased her troubled spirit. However, today, it did nothing to soothe her racing heart. Neither did the gentle breeze blow away the concern that threatened to overtake her. A light rustling through the trees as the zephyr swept over the farm and across the valley did remind her that just as the wind in due time would cease blowing and a stillness would prevail again, so would the turmoil she was feeling inside pass and a peace would once again settle in and over her.

Lingering on the bridge a while longer, Deborah allowed the thoughts of Malachi Hebron to take priority in her mind. *We were so young when you first came to Dotson Farm searching for Levi Taylor. We fell in love and both of us knew it was the real thing. The few times we have been together have always strengthened that bond, and when we are apart that love remains strong and solid. Like an anchor, it holds us steadfast and stable.*

Somewhere in the distance she heard a voice but couldn't bring herself back to the present. "Deb! Deb!"

She stood transfixed on the bridge, shutting out the voice. She wanted to stay lost in her memories a while longer, but the voice was persistent.

"Deb! Deborah Dotson! I know you hear me! Aren't you supposed to go into Pueblo? The carriage is ready and waiting!"

"Okay, Luke. Thanks. I'm coming." She gave her brother a wave and walked back over the bridge. Before getting into the carriage, she went around the side of the house to the back, walked across the veranda to the kitchen door and opened it enough to look inside just as Dorcas Dotson entered the kitchen. "I am leaving for Pueblo, Mawmaw. Is there anything you need from town?"

"No," Dorcas replied, walking to the door. "How long will you be gone?"

"I am not sure. It may be late, so don't worry." Deborah opened the door wider, stepped inside and gave her Mawmaw a big hug. "I love you, Mawmaw." For a brief moment, she clung to Dorcas.

Dorcas held her close. "I love you. Be very careful." Watching Deborah drive away in the carriage, she waved goodbye and uttered the words that always came to the forefront of her mind anytime either of the grandchildren were out of her sight. "You and Luke are all Pawpaw Silas and I have. Had it not been for you, we would not have survived the tragedy of losing our son and his wife so many years ago. I still do not understand why that had to be, but God knows best. I am so thankful, He left us you."

Arriving in Pueblo, Deborah parked the carriage in front of Dorsey's Store. Reaching inside her reticule, she took out a small locket. Opening it, with a smile she looked into a face that seemed to be smiling back at her. She kissed the tip of her forefinger then touched it to the picture of the young man. "Oh, Malachi," she whispered. "I wonder where you are and if you are safe. I haven't heard from you in a while. I understand, or at least I try to, but it is so hard not knowing. You told me not to worry, but I do worry." She snapped the locket closed, turned it over and read what she had so many times over the last four years. "Deb, you are the wings that keep me soaring. I love you, Malachi" She closed her eyes as sweetness of their love washed over her. Holding the locket close to her heart, she whispered, "There will never be anyone else for me, Malachi. I shall always love you and no one else. So don't you let anything happen to you lest I die an old maid."

"Deborah?"

She opened her eyes. "Oh....oh, Mr. Dorsey."

"I'm sorry. I must have startled you. Are you all right?"

"Yes sir. You did startle me, but I am all right, since it's you. I was lost in a memory, which at this time is not a good thing."

Mr. Dorsey grinned. "I thought memories of Malachi were always a good thing. For you, that is."

"Normally, it is. But to get so caught up in them and lose track of time and the reason I am here today is not wise." Opening the locket again and forcing her eyes to look at the small clock opposite the picture, she uttered, "Four thirty. The train should be arriving soon."

"In thirty minutes," Dorsey replied. "Hadn't you better come inside the store? I must get back. There are a couple of customers milling around."

Chapter 9

Deborah entered Dorsey's Store and rambled around briefly before focusing her eyes on a large clock hanging behind the counter where Mr. Dorsey conducted his business transactions.

Dorsey, also, glanced at the clock. "Deborah, is there something in particular you are interested in?"

"Well, not really. Maybe I should check your supply of milk for Pawpaw Silas and give him a report as to when it may need to be replenished."

Dorsey gave her a keen look. "Good idea. Go ahead to the storeroom. The milk vault is in there, at the back."

Entering the storeroom and trying to squelch the anxiety within her, Deborah walked around observing items that remained in the back unless a customer asked for them. While wandering around, she came across a well-worn bin cluttered with items. Deciding that would be a good way to keep her occupied, she piddled through the odds and ends and picked up a small, hard object. Walking to the window of the storeroom, she ran her finger over the item following the outline of its shape. Although a few small rough spots were visible, she knew it was solid through and through. "An anchor," she whispered. "You are very small, but it is what you represent that makes you valuable. Solid, firm and steadfast. Something that one can hold on to when being tossed and turned with the uncertainties of life."

Removing the locket from her reticule, she held it and the small anchor to her chest and stared out the window. The population of Pueblo, Colorado, had increased tremendously. New buildings lined the town square as a result of various merchants moving in, bringing a diversity of culture and business to the area. What once was referred to as the Village of Pueblo was now called the Town of Pueblo. She could still see the Colorado Mountains that formed the beautiful skyline of the town she loved. Even though some of the merchants offered interested and needful items, her favorite stores and places to shop were still Dorsey's Store and the Dressmakers's Shop where Mawmaw Dorcas displayed her home made quilts and doilies. Placing her other hand over the one holding the locket and anchor, Deborah pressed them tighter to her chest. "You are my anchor, Malachi. I need to see you. To feel my hand in yours. To feel you squeeze it. I need to hear you say, I love you, Deborah Dotson. Will you be my wife? Will you marry me? I know you have already said it, and I accepted, but somehow we seem to never be able to settle down long enough to make it happen. But one of these days…" She opened the locket and looked at the clock. "Oh, my! Five fifteen! I forgot all about the time."

The door opened and Mr. Dorsey stepped into the storeroom. "The train is running behind schedule, Deborah." He returned to the front, but shortly poked his head back through the door. "The train just passed and will be pulling into the station soon."

"Do you know who my contact is?"

"I have no idea. But I know the passcode. When the person arrives and gives the correct word, I will send your contact back here."

Deborah forced a smile as Mr. Dorsey closed the door. Pacing back and forth around the storeroom, her heart was pounding so hard it seemed it would burst open. She glanced at her small clock, again. *Five thirty. I need to head home. Pawpaw and Mawmaw will start to worry about me if I don't get back soon.*

Dorsey stood at the door of his store and watched as the train pulled away from the depot. He looked up and down the street observing passengers, some going one way and some another. He spotted what looked like a young man meandering along as if he hadn't a care in the world. *Wonder where he came from. A strange sort, to say the least. Could he have gotten off the train? Probably a stowaway.*

"Hmm. Oh, well." He walked toward the storeroom to inform Deborah that those who exited the train had paid no attention to him but went their own way. Hearing the bell above the door jingle, he turned as a strange looking fellow slouched into the store. *It's the street waif.* Dorsey took a few steps toward him, but the dawdler paid no attention.

"Can I help you with something?"

The straggler did not respond. Didn't even look his direction. He seemed to be ignoring Dorsey, then after a few minutes simply shook his head.

Dorsey was becoming a little suspicious and a lot cautious. "Well, if you need help just let me know." He walked behind the counter as another customer entered the store, picked up a sack of flour and a container of milk, paid for them and left, leaving only Dorsey and the straggler inside. Dorsey observed the young waif who was still wandering around the store. *He is all disheveled. His hat is about a size too large. His pants too short and that jacket is zipped all the way up to his neck. I guess it's a he. Could be a she.*

"Are you sure you don't want some help? If you are hungry, I can let you have something on credit." Dorsey glanced down at the small pistol under the counter.

The straggler looked around the store as if to be sure no other customers were around. Seemingly satisfied that they were alone and acting a little conspicuous, he walked toward Dorsey.

Dorsey reached down to pick up the pistol just as the stranger reached the counter.

"Good day, sir."

"Good...." Dorsey stopped when the straggler removed his hat and looked straight at him. "Uh....Malachi? What in the world?"

Malachi glanced around. "Shh. I am supposed to meet a contact here."

"You? You are the one?"

"I am." He grinned. "How do you like my disguise?"

Dorsey shook his head in disbelief. He chuckled. "Okay, but you still have to know the passcode."

"Aw, don't you trust me, Mr. Dorsey?"

"It is not a matter of trust, Malachi, but of obeying orders. Anyway your contact is in the storeroom wondering about you."

Malachi leaned over and whispered something in his ear.

"All right, you are for real. In there." He pointed to the door. As Malachi started to the storeroom, Dorsey asked, "By the way, do you know who your contact is?"

"I do not. Never had any business with him before."

Dorsey smiled. The bell above the door jingled and a customer walked inside the store. Turning his back to the storeroom, he uttered, "That's what you think, Malachi Hebron. Boy, are you ever in for a surprise."

Chapter 10

Hearing the door open, Deborah moved quickly from the window and stepped behind a nearby stack of boxes. She waited, barely daring to breathe. *In training, I learned when the contact comes to meet me, he must give the passcode first.*

Anxiously, Malachi stepped inside the storeroom. Closing the door quietly, he looked around but saw no one. He stood near the door and waited. Silence greeted him. Not a sound or movement let him know there was someone in the room. He knew how to be quiet and vigilant. Aso, he knew how to be light and swift on his feet which had saved his life many times. However, being shut up in a storeroom with someone he had never met and had no idea of that person's modus operandi brought an awareness of possible betrayal. But that came with the job. Taking chances, that is. Swift as a mouse, he took one step. He twiddled his thumbs and twitched his nose. *I know I am supposed to speak the passcode first, but not before I know there is really someone in here. It seems we are playing the waiting game. Oh well, I've done it before, and I can do it again, at least for a while.*

Deborah remained hidden behind the stack of boxes. *I know someone came in here. Maybe it is Mr. Dorsey. No, he would say something. It must be my contact. If he wants to play the waiting game, I can oblige him. Patience is a virtue that I have acquired, somewhat, during my twenty years. This is my first assignment, and I will not foul it up.* She waited, her thoughts turning to Malachi. *But, Malachi Hebron, my patience in waiting on you to settle down and marry me is being tested, tremendously. That is why I took this job. Won't you be surprised when I see you again. Who knows when that will be. I surely don't.* A shuffling noise jolted her back to the imminent moment. She trembled. Excitement and anxiety were closing in on her. Putting her arms across her chest and pressing tightly, she tried to calm her racing heart. *Patience, Deborah, patience.* Gradually the nervousness eased. She relaxed and waited for the contact to reveal himself.

Malachi was quite the opposite. By nature he was not a patient person. His job had taught him, at times it pays to be patient. However, he had learned at other times procrastination could be fatal. *I have waited long enough. This silence is wasting time, which I am not willing to do at this moment.* Moving about, he cleared his throat, grunted and shuffled his feet.

Deborah continued to stand very still. *Guess I could show myself.* Just as she started to move, she heard a voice.

"Okay. Mr. Dorsey said you are in here. If you are waiting for the passcode, I will not voice it until you come out of hiding and show your face. We have to know what each other looks like."

Surprised when her contact spoke, Deborah felt as if her feet were glued to the floor. *I know that voice. Malachi. It can't be. I was thinking of him so strongly until I am imaging he is here.* She could not bring herself to move. *It can't be him. Mr. Dorsey would have told me. Unless…,unless he didn't know.*

Malachi had run out of patience. "I don't have time to play hide and seek. This is urgent…" He was interrupted as a small female rushed out of seemingly nowhere flinging herself into his arms.

He held her close as she whispered, "Malachi."

He didn't speak. He relished the feel of her in his arms, realizing how much he had missed her.

Deborah stirred. He held her tighter. "Don't move. Let's stay like this forever."

Deborah relaxed again, momentarily. Then putting both hands on his chest, she looked up at him. "Oh Malachi." She moved but stayed in the circle of his arms.

"I love you Deborah Dotson. Will you…"

Deborah put her finger to his lips. "Don't say it, Malachi. Not now. Mr. Dorsey didn't tell you I was back here?"

He removed her finger but held onto her hand. "No. With this disguise, and I had my hat slouched down partially hiding my face, he didn't recognize me at first. And when I made myself known, he still didn't tell me. I am supposed to meet a contact here, and then I was going to the farm to see you. It is good that you chose this day to come into Pueblo. But what are you doing in the storeroom of Dorsey's Store?" Malachi got a strange look on his face as realization dawned. "Deb, you are not...." He stopped.

She smiled up at him and shook her head. "I am supposed to meet a contact here."

Malachi squeezed her to him, again. "No, Deb. No. Tell me it's not true. I will not let you. It is too dangerous. No. No. No."

Deborah remained in the circle of his arms. "I am not in any danger. I'm not considered an agent, yet."

"But I am. That is a well-known fact, not only in America, but also in other countries. If you are seen with me, agent or not, you are in grave danger until this mess I am involved in is cleared up." Malachi released her and walked over to the window.

Deborah followed. "I have some information for you, but you must give me the passcode."

Malachi turned and faced her with a mischievous grin. "Don't you trust me?"

"Yes. But this is government business. Orders are to trust no one until proven reliable and that includes you. We have to follow the rules."

"Did you know that I am your contact?"

"Of course not. I am never supposed to know. That is why the passcode is needed." Deborah opened her reticule and removed a small slip of paper. "This belongs to you."

Malachi reached out to take the paper from her. She smiled and put it behind her back. "Passcode, please."

"Okay. But first, this." He kissed her. "You will make a good agent. You are solid and steadfast. The passcode is...." Interrupted by a commotion at the storeroom door they both turned. "You stay here," Malachi whispered.

Still holding the slip of paper in her hand, Deborah waited as Malachi quietly, but quickly, eased over to the door. He heard arguing.

"I'm going in!" Stormed a strange voice.

"You are not!" Mr. Dorsey replied. "No one is allowed in my storeroom without my permission! And you do not have my permission!"

"I'm going in there if I have to knock you out and break down the door!"

"That will be the only way you get in! Go ahead and try if you are prepared to suffer the consequences!"

Knowing Mr. Dorsey was stalling his would be captor to give him ample time to escape, Malachi rushed to Deborah and took the slip of paper from her hand. Quickly removing the leather pouch from inside his jacket, he put the information in it and dropped the pouch back into its hiding place. He grabbed Deborah's hand. "Come on, Deb. We have to get out of here."

"But....but the passcode," she said as they rushed out the back door of the storeroom.

"Later," Malachi replied. "Right now, run Deborah Dotson, run. Run for your life."

Chapter 11

Running down the back alley of the storefront of Pueblo's busy section, Malachi and Deborah dodged empty boxes, trash bins and garbage that was scattered from one side to the other by stray animals or hobo's looking for a morsel of food. Pausing at the back of the Dressmaker's Shop to catch their breath, Malachi put his arm around Deborah. "Hadn't you better get back to the farm?"

"Yes. Pawpaw and Mawmaw will be so worried, but I don't want to leave you to face this alone."

"It is not me I'm worried about. It's you."

"But we are in this together."

"No, Deb. You must get back to the farm. You must not be seen with me." Malachi walked to the corner of a building. "Follow this narrow path to the storefront. Go in the Dressmaker's Shop and browse around awhile. Then go back to Dorsey's for the carriage. Do not tarry, Deb. Get home as fast as you can."

"I found something in the storeroom I wanted so I kept it. I must go back into the store and pay Mr. Dorsey." She removed the small, solid item from her reticule. "Give me your hand."

"Gladly."

Deborah placed the piece of iron into his hand and closed his fingers over it. "I want you to have this."

Malachi put both arms around her keeping his hand tightly closed. "I will try to get to the farm if I can do so without putting your family in danger. Now go."

Hurrying down the narrow alley, Deborah went straight to the Dressmaker's Shop. Too late. It was closed. Nonchalantly and with an occasional backward glance, she walked down the boardwalk to Dorsey's Store. Opening the door quickly, but before she could enter, a man came storming out, whamming into her so hard she stumbled backward. Without even a grunt, much less an excuse me, he stalked down the boardwalk in a rage, mumbling under his breath. Gaining her composure, Deborah watched the angry man turn at the corner of the building. "Oh," she whispered. "He is headed to the back alley. He is after Malachi. Run, Malachi, run." When she entered the store, Mr. Dorsey was helping a customer but turned his attention toward her. Their eyes locked. She gave him a smile and slight head nod.

"I will be with you when I finish up here, Deborah." When they were alone, Mr. Dorsey asked, "Malachi escaped?"

"Thanks to you, he did. But that man threatened you. Did we put you in danger?"

"Oh, no. Don't you worry about it."

"Malachi warned me not to tarry. I found an item mixed among some other trinkets in a bin in the storeroom so I need to pay for it."

"No charge. Sometimes I pick up things here and there that really do not have much value to most people. I just add them to that bin."

"I actually gave it to Malachi. It was a small anchor."

⚓⚓⚓

Malachi watched until Deborah turned at the corner of the building. Realizing he was still clutching tightly to whatever she had put into his hand, he slowly released his grip. "An anchor," he whispered. Looking down the alley, he was very tempted to cover the distance, find her and hold her close to him again. "You are like an anchor to me, Deborah Dotson, and don't you forget it. If something should happen to you, I would fall apart piece by piece."

Hurrying down the back alley, his eyes focused on a clearing that opened up into the town. Suddenly, he hit the ground with a thud landing flat on his face. Paying no attention to where he put his feet, he had stepped into a hole. "Ugh," he grunted, pushing himself up with both hands. "Of all places for a hole to be. I must have twisted my ankle." Limping a little, he looked back over his shoulder. He saw a shadow near the opening where he and Deborah had parted. Moving as fast as he could, he came to the clearing and ducked behind some fire wood that was stacked neatly beside the end building. Peeking over the top of the stack of wood, he saw the shadow hesitate before moving his direction. About to skedaddle, he waited as the shadow bent down and picked up something from the ground. *I wonder what he found.* Malachi patted his jacket and felt the leather pouch still secure in its hiding place. Then he remembered. *Oh, the anchor. I must have opened my hand during the fall and dropped it.*

Feeling a sharp pain from his ankle shoot up his leg, Malachi ducked back behind the stack of wood. Trying to put all his weight on the leg that wasn't hurting left him somewhat unbalanced. *I'm thankful the guy is following me for that lets me know he has not connected Deb to this assignment.* Trying to hurry from the wood pile to get out of town was in vain. He could barely creep along. *Okay, this will never work.* He pondered a moment. Casting another glance down the alley, he no longer saw the shadow. The fact that he had not seen which direction the man went, or if he was hiding among the rubbish, disturbed him greatly. Chastising himself, he uttered, "I can't do anything the way I am. I must get some help. One moment of carelessness and see where it landed you. Malachi Hebron, let this be a lesson to you. This job requires prudence, awareness and vigilance, continually. There is no room for negligence."

Limping his way to the storefront, by the time he reached the doctor's office, he could barely drag his wounded leg. Opening the door, he stumbled inside and sank slowly to the floor, blocking the entrance.

Someone was patting his cheek. He heard a voice that sounded very far away. "Malachi? Malachi, wake up."

Malachi stirred and opened his eyes. "Dr. White, what am I doing here?"

"I was with a patient and heard a noise. Excusing myself, I walked to the waiting area and found you blocking the doorway, out cold and crumpled on the floor in a heap."

Malachi flinched as the sharp pain shot up his leg. "Oh, yes. I stepped in a hole and twisted my ankle and leg. What a dumb thing to do."

Dr. White helped him to a chair. "Sit here until I finish with my patient and I'll check it out." Momentarily, the patient walked into the waiting room and with barely a glance in Malachi's direction exited the building.

Dr. White assisted him into a small room and upon the exam table. Malachi flinched as the doctor poked around on his ankle and foot. "The severe sprain in your ankle is causing the pain to shoot up your leg. The ankle needs a cast."

"Oh no, Dr. White, no cast. Just bind it up tightly and give me something to ease the pain. I have to get away from here."

"Okay. It is definitely not the wisest thing to do. It is against my better judgment, but if that is what you want."

Malachi was fidgety as the doctor wrapped a binding around his ankle. "Hold still, Malachi. Can't you relax for a few minutes?"

"No sir, I can't, Doc. I must get away from here before I get you in trouble."

After binding the ankle, Dr. White asked, "What kind of trouble? What is going on, Malachi?

Malachi frowned and flinched as another pain pierced his leg. The doctor handed him a cup of water and offered him a pill.

"Wait a minute. Is that going to make me sleepy?"

"Uh, probably, maybe a little drowsy."

"Then I am not swallowing it. I don't have time to be drowsy, much less sleep."

Dr. White stared at him. "I will ask you again. What is going on? I am not dumb or blind. I saw Deborah leaving town earlier as if fleeing a fire. What was she running from? Deborah doesn't drive a team like that without good cause. I am your doctor. You can trust me, Malachi."

Malachi tried to get off the exam table. "Help me, Dr. White."

"You need to heed my advice and stay off that ankle for a few days."

"It is not a matter of not trusting you, Doc. I learned to trust you when you took such good care of Levi while he was staying at the Dotson farm, and your friendship with the family proved to me you are reliable. It's just, well, I don't want you to be in danger."

"I am your physician, now. As my patient, I have a right to know what is troubling you."

Malachi looked at him. "I'm," he paused. "I am a government agent."

"I know."

"You do? Without my knowledge, Deborah goes and gets herself involved in government business."

"I know that, too."

"Do her grandparents and Luke know?"

"They know she has a part time job with intelligence, but they do not know to what extent. She doesn't want them to know that what she does has some risk to it."

Malachi smiled. "What else do you know?"

"I know that you are on a double assignment."

"You do?" Malachi ran his fingers through his hair. "You and Mr. Dorsey. Well, I'll be. Wonders never cease. I found out about Mr.

Dorsey shortly before coming to Pueblo. I had to tell him the passcode before meeting with my contact. I surely didn't know about you."

"Guess I'm, well, shall we say, your ace in the hole."

Chapter 12

When the book she had been reading slipped from her lap onto the floor, Deborah awakened with a start. Darkness covered her like a shroud. Sitting up straight, she gripped the arms of the chair in a desperate effort to squelch the tingling sensation brought on by the eerie blackness of her bedroom and the feeling that something was amiss. *I don't remember falling asleep in the chair. Neither do I remember turning off the lantern. Guess my sleepless nights have caught up with me.* She sat alert and listened. There was no noise coming from the hall or downstairs so she closed her eyes and rested her head against the back of the chair. Events of the previous day flooded her mind.

"Malachi," she breathed. A wash of terror overwhelmed her. She could not dispel the nagging feeling that he was in trouble. Turning on the lantern, she picked it up and stepped out of her bedroom, quietly closing the door. Switching the lantern off and tiptoeing down the hall, she paused at Luke's door. The only sound she heard was his loud snoring. Proceeding to the top of the stairs, she didn't need a light to keep from toppling downward. Having gone up and down those stairs since she was old enough to do so, even in the darkness she knew where to put her feet. Holding onto the stair rail, she descended with ease.

Putting the lantern on the kitchen table, Deborah poured some milk into a glass and sat down. With both hands around the partially filled glass, she stared at a picture on the kitchen wall close to the exit door. It was not in a frame but was painted on a smooth piece of lumber. Many times she had gone through that door and not paid any attention to the thing that now captivated her. Maybe it was because of the restlessness of the past week and the uneasy feeling that kept troubling her. Whatever the reason, the picture seemed to come alive. A small boat was tossing on turbulent waves of stormy waters. Below the boat the water was clear. She saw a line going downward. It was attached to an anchor resting on the bottom of the sea. Although the small vessel was swerving and tossing on the mighty waves, the anchor was holding it secure. Words to the right of the boat appeared to step from the wood and walk into her heart. *The Anchor holds in spite of the storm.*

Leaving her untouched milk on the table, Deborah picked up the lantern and walked to the back door. Pausing beside the picture, she looked at the words then at the boat that was tossing on the turbulent waves. Focusing on the words she whispered, "The Anchor holds, in spite of the storm." Stepping onto the veranda, the words were burning in her heart. "It feels as if a storm is raging inside of me. Just hope I can stay secured to the Anchor."

She stood in the darkness with only her thoughts as company which were not too comforting at the moment. Staring in the direction of the fruit and nut orchard, thanks to a small amount of moonlight, she could make out the tree line. The fact there had been no word from Malachi had her vacillating with fear. *It has been more than a day since we parted in the back alley at Pueblo. I thought you would come to the farm, but....* A movement in the orchard caught her eye and interrupted her thoughts. She whispered, "Could someone be snooping around? Something is stirring out there." Hearing a noise, the orchard had her undivided attention as she stepped to the edge of the veranda and pressed her face against the screen. She listened intently but did not hear anything. "I am certain I heard something. Oh well, maybe just a temporary rustling of leaves as the wind bristles through the trees." Knowing she should march right back into the kitchen and up to bed, she sighed. "The only thing, what I should do and what I am compelled to do definitely are not in agreement. With this storm raging inside of me, I am apt to do most anything."

Opening the screen door of the veranda, she walked down the steps. *The Anchor holds, in spite of the storm.* With the words from the picture echoing in her mind, taking a deep breath, cautiously and determined, she walked to the orchard. Turning the lantern on dim, although a bit perplexed, she made her way among the trees. The shiver she felt was not caused from the mountain air or the slight breeze that was sweeping through the orchard, but from the cold chill bumps that were crawling up and down her spine and arms. She turned the lantern off and stood very still hoping if someone was there, they would make a move. Nothing. Turning the lantern back on, a scary thought overwhelmed her. *That was a dumb thing to do, Deborah Dotson. If an unwelcome visitor is among the trees, you could be...*

Another shiver interrupted her thoughts. "With this small lantern, I can't really find anything tonight that would let me know someone was actually here, or if it was only my imagination. I will look it over good tomorrow. Anyway, it will be to my advantage to go to the house." Stepping out of the orchard into the clearing, like a magnet her eyes were drawn toward the stables. Knowing it would be wise to get back to the house and safety, she argued with herself, but only momentarily. "This is a mind over matter situation." Turning the lantern up a notch, she started toward the stables. "I have a mind to do it and at this moment, well, I'll have to suffer the consequences of the matter if it is the wrong thing."

She dared a quick glance back toward the house, knowing if Pawpaw Silas couldn't sleep and was in the kitchen he would, no doubt, step onto the veranda to breathe the mountain air and would see her light. Determined to satisfy her curiosity, she hurriedly made her way to the stables. Stepping inside, spooky chill bumps crawled up and down her spine again. *It is eerie in here.* She stood as if frozen, afraid to move. *Scaredy cat. You are not so brave after all.* Sure that she heard a noise inside the stable, Deborah realized she could move and did so quickly. She hurried over to the stall where her horse, Beauty, was munching hay, leaned over the rail of the stall and laid her hand on the mare's head. Beauty lifted her head and nuzzled her owner's face. Deborah hung the lantern on the rail, put both arms around the mare's neck and laid her face against Beauty's head. "You won't let anybody hurt me, will you, Beauty?" The mare neighed with reassurance of her devotion and protection.

After removing the lantern from the rail and patting Beauty again, Deborah decided to check on Zero, Luke's horse, before leaving the stables. Taking the few steps to the stall and seeing Zero was beyond her reach, she decided it best not to linger any longer. Trying to maneuver her way with only the dim light of the lantern, she ran smack dab into a partially filled feeding bucket that Luke had carelessly left unattended. Falling face down, she landed on some loose hay which softened the blow, somewhat, but the lantern flew from her hand, hit the rail of a stall and shattered into bits and pieces. With small fragments of glass scattered all around her, she lay still, trying to gather her wits. "Oh, Luke," she breathed, "you did it again. That's the third time this week you have not emptied the feeding bucket and put it back where it belongs. It is getting to be a habit."

Managing to get to her feet in the pitch blackness, she brushed at the loose straw that she knew was clinging to her clothes. "I am not hurt, no thanks to you, my dear brother. However, I do feel like my brain is a bit rattled." She heard Beauty neigh. Still somewhat discombobulated, she took a step toward the horse but stopped cold when a strong arm grabbed her around the waist. Before she could let out a scream, a hand clamped over her mouth. Without a sound from her assailant, she felt herself being pulled into the darkness.

Knowing her captor was the stronger, she did not kick her legs or flail her arms in an effort to break loose from his hold, realizing resistance would be only wasted energy. While her assailant did not seem to be in a hurry, Deborah's mind was racing like a freight train. *You are not moving very fast, whoever you are. My ninety seven pounds must be pretty heavy. I will bide my time. My opportunity will come. You cannot go on like this forever.*

Her chance came as she knew it would. Her captor loosened the hand that covered her mouth, not much but just enough. She clamped down on it with her teeth. *That should do it.* To her surprise, he didn't utter a sound. *I know I felt him flinch. What's wrong with him. Surely he has a voice.*

Chapter 13

Dorcas Dotson eased out of bed and walked softly out of the room so not to awaken Silas. Picking up the lantern that occupied a table near the door, with bare feet she patted across the floor and made her way to the foot of the stairs. Flipping the lantern switch to dim, she ascended the stairs to do what she had done every night for the past thirteen years, to check on her grandchildren. It was habit but one she loved and would greatly miss when the time came for them to leave home. Opening the door to Luke's room, there was no need to shine the light inside as his not too soft breathing let her know he was in bed and asleep. She smiled. *Luke, you are not even quiet when you are sleeping.*

Making her way down the hall, she opened the door to Deborah's room. All was quiet and still. She held the lantern out in front of her and glanced around. A book was on the floor. *Hmm, that is not like Deborah.* Stepping quietly into the room, she titled the light toward the bed. The coverlet and sheet were turned down but Deborah was not there and from all appearances, she had not been in bed at all. Quickly making her way back down the stairs and into the kitchen, she noticed the glass partially filled with milk but saw no one. Turning the lantern up, puzzled, she whispered, "Deborah?" When there was no reply she spoke louder. "Deborah?" Opening the door to the veranda and holding the lantern higher, she asked, "Deborah, where are you?" Not receiving a response, concern and anxiety gripped her. Rushing from the kitchen back into the bedroom, she grabbed hold of her husband's shoulder giving it a good shake. "Silas, Silas, wake up. Deborah is not in her bed."

Silas stirred. "What? What is it, Maw? What's the matter?"

"Get up. Deborah is not in her bed."

"Well, she probably couldn't sleep, so went to the kitchen for some milk."

"No. The milk is on the table, but there is no sign of Deborah. Get out of that bed and do something."

"Okay. Okay. Maybe she wandered to the stables to check on Beauty. You know she does that sometimes. Hand me my clothes. Hadn't you better put something on over that gown before we go outside?"

Donning her robe, Dorcas followed Silas from the bedroom, down the hallway and into the kitchen. "Oh, we didn't get the pistol."

"We don't need the pistol," Silas replied.

Pausing in front of the buffet, Dorcas opened a drawer, took out a small pistol and handed it to Silas. "You don't know that for sure."

Silas gave her a lopsided grin, took the pistol and dropped it into his pants pocket. "You are right, as always." A look of concern wiped the grin from his face. "You really are worried, aren't you?"

"Yes, I am." Slipping her feet into some shoes she kept by the door, Dorcas followed him out of the house, handed the lantern to him and grabbed hold of his free hand. "Do you think we should check in the orchard?"

"I don't think Deborah would be rambling around in the orchard in the middle of the night. Do you?"

"I don't know what to think, Silas. I am fearful something has happened to her. Maybe she fell and hurt herself, or…" Her voice trailed off.

Silas squeezed her hand. "Let's check the stables first. We will probably find her curled up on some hay beside Beauty. She has slept in the stables before."

"Not in a long time, Silas, and you know it." Temporary silence prevailed as they made their way toward the stables.

"She's all right," Silas said, giving his wife's hand another squeeze. "Deborah is very prudent. She can be discreet and shrewd if it becomes necessary."

Silas entered the stables with Dorcas close behind him. They walked straight to Beauty's stall. Lifting the lantern over the rail, they looked all around the stall for a sign that Deborah may have been there. "I don't see anything unusual, do you?"

"No," Dorcas whispered, "but that doesn't mean she hasn't been here." When Silas lifted the lantern back over the rail, she glanced around the area near the stall. The reflection from the light revealed a shiny fleck amidst some loose straw. She walked over to the object, bent down and picked it up. *It's glass.* "Oooooh," escaped her lips.

"What is it?" Silas asked.

"Come…come over here with the light." She held the piece of glass closer to the lantern. "Look at this."

Silas took the glass but didn't say a word. Moving about the stable and turning the flame of the lantern up, they saw bits and pieces of glass and metal scattered over the floor, on top of straw and up against the railing. Growing concern gripped them.

Silas picked up a piece of metal. "It's from Deborah's lantern. It is a miracle the stables didn't catch on fire with all this hay about."

"But where is Deborah? And how did she happen to break the lantern?"

"Don't panic. Let's check on Zero and look around some more. Maybe we will find out where and how. Be careful. Don't step on any of the broken pieces. Luke and I can clean this mess up in the morning."

Maneuvering over broken glass, they moved about looking around and upward for some clarification of the matter. Silas stumbled causing a loud vibrating noise when his foot hit something solid. He bent down. "Here's the how. Luke did it again."

"That boy," Dorcas said when she saw the overturned bucket. "Yes, Deborah was here, and no doubt she tripped over the bucket, fell and the lantern broke." Overwhelmed by anxiety, she grabbed hold of Silas. "Oh, but Silas, where is she now?"

"Good question. Try not to worry." He put an arm around her. "Let's check inside the stables some more before going back outside."

They went from one stall to the other, searching diligently. Handing the lantern to Dorcas, Silas removed a pitch fork that was hanging on a nail of a support post. Carefully, he stuck the fork into some hay that was stacked over in a corner of the stable.

"If she is in there, I do hope you don't poke that pitch fork into her," Dorcas said.

Silas looked at her. "Now, Maw, pull yourself together. Don't you know if I thought she was in the hay, I wouldn't be poking into it with a sharp pitch fork? No, I do not expect to find her hidden in the stack of hay. I'm just checking it out." Poking around in the pile, he scattered hay about until sure nothing was there that would let them know Deborah had been forced to hide in the stack for a spell. Satisfied that she was not in that stable and letting Dorcas carry the lantern, Silas kept the pitch fork as that walked through a doorway and entered the other stable. Searching it carefully they found nothing and the only noise they heard was the sound of horses munching hay.

Exiting through the rear door, Silas put the pitch fork against the stable and took the lantern. Reconsidering, he reached back and removed the fork from its place and handed it to Dorcas. "On second thought, maybe we had better take it along."

"But you have the pistol. You will use it if you have to?"

"Only if I have to. I don't won't to kill somebody unless it is absolutely necessary."

"Well, if someone has hurt my granddaughter, and we find him, it will become absolutely necessary."

"Okay. Let's look around outside before moving on."

Finding nothing near the stables and with Dorcas right on his heels, Silas followed the well-worn path from the stables to the dairy barn. Stopping frequently, he moved the lantern around and with the help of a few stars and limited light from the moon, he was able to observe the area close to the path. Nearing the dairy barn they noticed some of the cows seemed restless.

"Wonder what is troubling the cows?" Dorcas asked.

"Could be a cougar near or…."

They both took off running as a blood curdling scream penetrated the night and echoed through the darkness.

Chapter 14

Deborah sat on a milking stool inside the dairy barn. "I am sorry I bit you, Malachi. Does it hurt very badly?"

"Well, uh, let's say that you have very sharp teeth. I haven't been bitten by a female since Anna and I were little." He chuckled. "When I would pester her, as older brothers do, her only defense was to bite me."

"Give me your hand."

Malachi was sitting on the floor of the barn near the stool. "Gladly," he said, putting the lantern down between them.

She took his hand and held it close to the dim light. "Wow. I brought blood. That must have been painful."

He leaned over close to her face. "A kiss would have felt better. Much, much better." Deborah kissed his hand. Grinning, he said, "That's not quite what I had in mind. Besides, didn't you recognize the feel of my arm? Or have you been allowing other men to put an arm around you in my absence?"

Deborah ignored his playful manner. "Malachi Hebron, this is not a time to be funny. Your life is in danger. You should have let me know it was you. I couldn't see a thing in the dark. Thanks to Luke and my carelessness. I should have paid more attention to what was on the stable floor instead of straining my eyes to see if someone was swinging from the ceiling beams. Fortunately, I could make my way around the stable without a light." She paused. "Did you hear something?"

"Shh," Malachi said in a whisper. They listened intently. "Probably just the cows. They are restless tonight."

"Why didn't you let me know it was you?" Deborah whispered.

"Because, number one, I didn't expect to find you wandering around the stable in the middle of the night without a light. Number two, when I realized it was you, I knew you were in as much danger as I am if I was being trailed."

"Why didn't you come to the house? You were just going to leave without seeing me?"

"I had planned to stay in the stables tonight just in case I was followed and go to the house in the morning. I tried to be discreet and be sure no one was pursuing me, but one can never be too careful."

"But if you weren't followed, and even if you were, we would have hidden you."

"No, Deb, I didn't want to risk getting your family involved in this matter and expose you to danger, but it seems I have done just that. The very thing I tried not to do. I should not have come here."

"Oh Malachi, don't say that. I am already involved. The job I took is bound to put me at some risk. All seems quiet and okay to me."

"Well, I thought so at first, but just about the time I entered the stable from the back, you walked in. Knowing the stable would be the first place an assailant would look, I had to get you out of there. Feeling the dairy barn would be safer, I got you here as quickly as possible."

"You weren't moving very fast. Am I that heavy?"

"No," Malachi, whispered. "It is nothing."

"It is nothing? What is nothing? What happened?"

"I had a little accident after we parted in the alley." He hushed. "Shh."

After a period of silence, Deborah whispered, "The cows are more restless than usual."

"Yes. There must be someone out there middling around. Is Articus in his pen?"

"Articus? He is. However, no one with a sound mind would go near him."

Still speaking in hushed tones, Malachi replied, "Good. I have a plan. I am going out there." He got up from his place on the barn floor and headed to the door.

"Malachi, you are limping."

He stopped. "I'm okay. Just a sprained ankle. Doc White fixed me up. It will be all right."

"What are you going to do? With that hurt ankle you can't move fast enough to get away from Articus when he gets stirred up."

"I believe someone is out there. I am going to let Articus out of his pen. When I do, you take off running to the house as fast as you can. Do not look back. I will, with the help of Articus, and if my plan doesn't backfire on me, steer the unwelcome visitor away from here. Sure hope Luke won't be too mad when he has to round up a raving, raging bull."

"But, Malachi, what about you?"

"If all seems safe and clear, I'll come back here and we will go to the house. Otherwise, you will know when Articus is free. You do what I say, Deb."

"How will I know if you are safe?"

Malachi held her close. "If I can do it without putting your family in danger, I will come back later. If not, I'll get word to you someway. I will be safe." He could feel the pounding of her heart. Strangely, that helped to calm his fears and ease the pounding of his own heart. "I love you. You are the wings that keep me soaring, Deborah Dotson. Don't you forget it." He released her, picked up a pail, put some grain in it and stepped out of the barn.

Deborah followed him. Placing the grain bucket on the ground, he grabbed her by both shoulders, picked her up and put her back inside. "When you know Articus is loose, and you hear the commotion, you get to the house. Can you find your way without a lantern?"

"I can. I love you, Malachi." Deborah watched him move quietly and quickly as possible while hobbling on an injured ankle. Maneuvering his way, he moved farther and farther into the blackness. She could barely make out his form with only the light of a few twinkling stars, and a small moonbeam that stretched from sky to earth.

Malachi stealthily made his way from the dairy. Ducking frequently behind a scrubby tree or a bush, he was aware the cows had gotten even more agitated. Nevertheless, knowing the safest way was to intermingle among them, he made his way closer to the pen where Articus was. *I have a creepy feeling that someone is out there lurking in the darkness.* He heard a low, grunting growl coming from Articus that verified his suspicion. *Now I know for a fact, someone is out there.* Realizing there was not time to even consider turning back, he eased over to the gate where the bull was penned. *Hope my plan doesn't backfire on me. Jesus, you know I can't move very fast, so don't leave me on my own.* Holding the bucket of grain inside the pen, he put his hand on the gate and flipped the latch. Knowing he had to get Articus to the gate, he gave the railing a couple of hard raps with the metal pail. With his other hand, he held the lantern up and out and waited. No movement in the distance verified the fact that someone was out there. Yet, a tingling dread let him know there was.

Swinging the lantern back and forth and beating the pail against the gate to the tempo of twinkle, twinkle little star, he whistled the tune of the familiar nursery rhyme. In his peripheral vision, he could see the big bull heading his way. Then there it was. A shadow moving about. Whistling a little louder, he glanced back at Articus. The bull was moving faster, almost at a run. He kept swinging the lantern as the form of a man headed toward him. Malachi knew it was time for action.

"Okay, whoever you are. I give up. Come and get me." As his assailant came into view, he dropped the bucket of grain and gave the gate a hard push so that it opened wide enough for the huge animal to run through. To his relief, Articus was in full speed and tromped over the bucket of grain. Before he could even say a word, the ferocious bull, with head bowed and horns ready, headed toward the man in the distance. Taking advantage of the opportunity to move from the bull's pen into the darkness and make his escape, Malachi didn't waste time looking back. He knew his enemy, if he had any sense at all, was running in the opposite direction. Hearing a hysterical howl, Malachi chuckled. "Thanks Articus. I owe you an extra bucket of grain."

Deborah was standing just inside the door of the dairy barn. She heard Malachi whistling and the low clanging of the feeding pail as it vibrated against the pen gate. She shivered at the sound of an angry, blowing snort and the pounding of a heavy gargantuan animal that shook the barn and the ground beneath her feet. Then she heard it. Rushing out the door of the barn, she ran toward the stable as a blood curdling scream charged the atmosphere.

"Jesus, please keep Malachi safe. You are our solid Rock, our Anchor. You hold us steadfast and secure." Praying as she ran, she saw a light through blurry vision. She stumbled and fell. Then strong arms picked her up and held her close. With tears streaming down her face, she whispered, "Oh, Pawpaw, Pawpaw. It's Malachi. He is in danger."

Chapter 15

Listening to the pounding hooves of Articus, Malachi hobbled along without direction. With the sound of the magnificent beast ringing in his ears, he shivered at the shaking of the earth that would frighten the bravest of brave as each heavy stomp of the angry beast vibrated the ground where he walked. He wasn't sure, however, but what it was the pounding of his heart and the shaking of his own body that he felt. Trying to run, but to no avail, he held tightly to his pistol and limped along dragging his injured ankle. With only a small ray of light, he could barely see two feet in front of him. A cloud threatened to conceal the moon and steal even that tiny gleam, leaving him with only the spooky blackness as a companion. Finally, he came upon a large tree, almost running smack dab into it. No longer able to ignore the severe pain shooting up his leg, he sank to the ground and the huge ponderosa pine seemed to swallow up his thin frame.

Exhausted, he gladly welcomed the place of refuge. His breathing was shallow. He leaned back taking deep breaths forcing air back into his lungs. With the huge tree as a shelter and surrounded by darkness, he felt it was safe enough to linger. Weary and fighting drowsiness, he whispered, "I hope Articus doesn't catch the intruder. I really don't want to be responsible for another's death." Feeling himself slumping to the ground, with a jerk he sat up straight and forced his eyes open. Everything was quiet. No pounding hooves, no screaming, even the ground had ceased to quake. "My intention was just to scare the man away from Deb. Oh, well, guess if it had to be, better him than me." With fading voice, he surrendered to the power of slumber.

Malachi wasn't sure if it was his growling stomach brought on by hunger pangs or the constant pain in his leg that aroused him. Feeling a cramp in his side, he opened his eyes and realized he was no longer in a sitting position but slumped over sideways on the ground. "Ooh," he groaned, pushing himself up to a sitting position. Immediately reaching inside his shirt, he breathed a sigh of relief. Patting the leather pouch and getting a tighter grip on the pistol that hung loosely in his hand, he tried to stand. Pushing against the ground with all the strength he could muster up was not getting the job done. He tried again and again with no success. "This is getting me nowhere, but at least it banished the cramp in my side." Managing to maneuver his body and get on his knees, he pushed against the colossal tree with both hands and eased himself up, dropping the pistol in the process.

"Guess I better wander around to see if there is a body lying somewhere nearby or any sign of Articus." Bending down and picking up the pistol, he was very conscious of the severe pain in his leg. Nevertheless, as the morning sun edged its way above the mountain peak, he limped along. Thinking he was headed to the path Articus had taken when released from the pen, being somewhat disoriented, he was actually going in the opposite direction. The pain in his leg had quickly gone from severe to critical. Feeling weak and faint, he pushed forward. With strained effort, he uttered, "Malachi Hebron, you have really gotten yourself into a mess. But..but..can't stop…must go..on.." By this time his head was swimming and his stomach was doing somersaults. He felt his body swaying. He was going down, down, down, and with a thud hit the hard earth.

⚓⚓⚓

Luke followed Silas into the kitchen. "What's this all about Pawpaw?" He paused at the sight of Deborah. "Why, Deb, what are you doing here? You up and stirring this early? Wonders never cease," he teased.

Standing by the exit door with eyes focused on the motto hanging beside it, Deborah didn't even acknowledge their presence.

Silas put a hand on Luke's arm to still and quieten him then walked over to Deborah. "You okay?"

Deborah turned and fell against his chest. "Oh Pawpaw," she wept. "What if Articus killed Malachi."

Silas held her close. "Now, now, you know Malachi can take care of himself. He is very capable. His reflexes are top notch and he is as sly and cunning as a fox if the need arises."

"But he was hurt. Articus could have gone after him instead of the intruder. He…he may be dead by now."

Luke was beside himself. "Jumping Jehoshaphats! What's going on? Deb, Pawpaw, what about Articus, intruder, Malachi? How come I don't know about this? You know I love a mystery. I can solve it. Didn't I solve the mystery of Levi Taylor? Give me the details. All I know is Articus is out of his pen, and I've got to help find the big old beast."

Silas released Deborah. "Come on Luke. I'll give you some details outside. Deborah, you stay here."

"Pawpaw, I want to go. I am so worried about Malachi. I'm falling apart."

Silas put one hand on her shoulder and the other on the motto. "What do you see here, child?"

"A boat tossing and turning on the angry billows. My insides are tossing and turning just like that."

"Read the words, Deborah."

Deborah took a deep breath. "The Anchor holds, in spite of the storm."

"Who is your Anchor, Deborah?"

"Malachi."

"Malachi is strong and capable. But Malachi is not infallible. He is human, just as you are. For obvious reasons, the artist did the painting so the anchor could be seen. In reality an anchor is not seen. Malachi is attached to something the eye cannot see, but he knows it is there holding him steadfast. You are attached to Malachi, that is why you feel he is your anchor. You, like Malachi, must be attached to *The Anchor*. Jesus is the Anchor that will hold, when the angry waves of circumstances beyond your control are tossing and turning you like a boat on troubled waters."

"I know, Pawpaw. It is just so hard."

"Try not to worry. All will be well. Come on, Luke."

The men had not gotten far from the house when they heard Deborah's voice.

"Pawpaw, I don't want to disobey you, but I must help. I can look for Malachi while you and Luke search for Articus and for signs of the intruder."

"Okay. Come on. We won't call it disobedience. Let's just say you are using the Dotson stubbornness and persistence."

Luke gave his sister a hug. "Don't you worry, Sis. We'll work this out together."

Deborah put both arms around her brother. "Thank you, Luke. I appreciate it. You are a big help."

Luke laughed. "I mean it."

"So do I." They walked together until reaching the bull's pen. The three stared at the spilled bucket of grain and the trampled grass that had been crushed by the weight of their lost master of the pasture.

"Jumping Jehoshaphats!" Luke stepped onto a print of smashed grass. "Wow! What a foot!"

Silas and Luke followed the bull's prints leading them away from the pen. Deborah walked along the fence line observing the area around her. Venturing away from the wire, she followed a path often used to herd the milk cows from the pasture to the dairy barn. Making her way to the huge ponderosa pine that she had sat under many times while reading a good book, she stopped for a while and looked up through the towering branches of the gigantic tree. "Malachi, I pray you escaped from the man who is after you and from Articus. When he gets mad, he will rip a body to shreds." Picking up her search again, only mere seconds passed before she halted. "I heard something." She stood quietly and waited. Not hearing the noise again, meticulously, she resumed her search. "Maybe just tree limbs swaying in the wind." She stopped. "I know I heard something. That is not the rustling of branches. Sounded like a groan." Her eyes roved the area. Shading them with her hand, she saw something not far beyond. "It is a groan, and it's coming from whatever or whoever is on the ground. Malachi!" She ran to the form and dropped to her knees. "Malachi, oh Malachi." As she lifted his head, he let out another groan. She patted his face. "Malachi, it's me, Deborah."

Malachi opened his eyes. "Oh.. Deb.., I tried to get away, but this ankle and leg are too painful and won't support me. So…so..sorry."

Gently putting his head down, she got to her feet. "I will get help. Pawpaw and Luke are out looking for Articus. I won't be long." Deborah ran across the pasture yelling with every breath. "Pawpaw! Luke! I found Malachi! He can't walk! Come help me!"

Chapter 16

"Okay Malachi, you can go back to work. The next time you have an injury, obey your doctor and stay put until it heals, at least somewhat. Especially, if it is as vital as an ankle or leg."

"I know, Doc, but I was in a hurry to get the rest of the information I need and return to Washington. What I have obtained thus far is of utmost importance to the President."

Dr. White let his spectacles drop down to the tip of his nose. Looking over the rim of the glass, he gave the young man a stare. Although he said nothing, the look was worth a thousand words.

Malachi hung his head. "Yes sir, I agree. I have wasted more time by not listening to you than if I had postponed traveling a few days and allowed my ankle and leg to heal."

Dr. White removed his glasses and dropped them inside the pocket of his physician's coat. "Well, it has been said a bought experience is the best teacher. Not sure I completely agree with that philosophy. A bought experience can be very painful and costly. A person can be spared a lot of hard knocks and disappointments simply by listening and taking advice from the voice of one who has already traveled that road."

Malachi grinned. "Yes sir. I know I'm hardheaded and stubborn at times. Not that I think I am invincible, it is just, well, the Hebron determination and tenacity come out in times of decisions."

"All well and good, but sometimes determination and tenacity can get you in deep trouble if the situation is not carefully considered beforehand. It can even get a person killed."

"Now you sound like Papa. I had better get to the depot."

"Is Deborah waiting outside?"

"No sir. I insisted she go on back to the farm."

"Good. There was a stranger in here last week. I treated him for bruises and cuts, and his clothes were torn in several places."

"Did he say anything?"

"Not much. I questioned him, trying to stay discreet. He was pretty tight lipped. Said he had been hunting in some woods and a bear got after him. After falling several times while fleeing, according to his story, he managed to scamper up a tree. Just in time it seemed."

Malachi laughed out loud. "A bear, huh? No, not a bear. It was a bull."

Dr. White chuckled. "I thought as much. A peculiar sort of fellow." Reaching over to a small table that held medical supplies, the doctor picked up a small item. "He tried to pay for my services with this. When I refused, he dug in his pocket and pulled out a wad of bills. Before he left, he laid this on the table and told me to keep it. It wasn't worth anything to him. Pawn shop wouldn't give him two cents for it. Said he found it on the ground in the back alley." Dr. White handed the item to Malachi. "You may want it."

"My anchor! Deb gave this to me. I dropped it when I stepped in that hole and fell."

"I was told that the man was hanging around here yesterday inquiring about a Malachi Hebron. He was caught snooping around Dorsey's Store, and someone even spied him sticking his head inside my waiting room. I didn't see him. I was with a patient."

"Really? You think he is still here?"

The doctor followed Malachi outside. "I don't know. Abner, who owns the livery, told me the man bought a horse and rode out of town late yesterday afternoon. He could still be close by. You be careful. Do not step in any more holes and don't go and get yourself killed." Dr. White watched as the young man, in a fast trot, headed for the depot. "No doubt he had some good principles put in him growing up, but youth can be so reckless. Sometimes I wonder if the young are afraid of anything."

Malachi leaned back in the seat as the train carried him to his next important meeting with government officials. However, it was not the meeting or his destination that was forefront in his mind, but it was that horrible night when he had arrived at the Dotson farm. In retrospect, he knew he had been followed by someone who desperately wanted to get his hands on the information that was hidden in the leather pouch concealed inside his shirt. He sat up straighter in the seat. *I have a feeling the man not only wanted the information, but he also wanted to do away with the carrier of the information. I shudder to think that the full life I have planned for Deborah and me could have been wiped out by such a lawless person. Thanks to Articus, the man didn't accomplish his mission.* He chuckled. *My, was that humungous beast ever mad.*

With an occasional jolt as the train rumbled over unlevel tracks carrying Malachi closer to his destination, he recalled how Silas and Luke had rounded up Articus and put him back into the pen. In their search they saw human tracks that led to a tree, the only sign that someone had been snooping around. *He must have been very quick and shrewd to outwit that bull. Hopefully, Articus put enough fear into him so the Dotsons won't be bothered with the him again.* He thought of Deborah, her sweetness and concern. "I love you, Deborah Dotson," he whispered. "One of these days you are going to marry me and…"

He held his breath while the train crossed the rickety rails spanning a narrow gorge over Clear Creek Canyon that towered above Georgetown, Colorado. He exhaled deeply as it finally started a descent carrying him down a steep slope to a green valley, then back up again. Weaving its way through the Rocky Mountains, Malachi held onto the seat of the Union Pacific as the train never slowed down but kept up full speed while swerving and wavering on the edge of a rocky cliff drop off. It coasted back down into another valley where beautiful twisting streams could be seen and enjoyed, if a traveler had time to spare. Of which, he had none.

Continuing west the rails twisted over and around the great sand dunes of eastern Utah. Malachi marveled that the bottom portion of some of the dunes had already been preserved into huge sandstones. He was amazed how the great stones varied in appearance, caused by the combination of pieces of rocks and minerals that were cemented together with crushed grains of sand. He finally relaxed as the rails turned northward crossing over Utah Lake and carrying him through another valley with its lush springs and wetlands. After several days of traveling, the train pulled into the depot at Promontory City, Utah, bringing him to his destination. Picking up his travel bag, he exited the train. Of all the days of traveling and stopping at various towns, he had seen no one who seemed to be haunting his trail yet knew there could always be someone lurking nearby. Standing on the platform of the rail station, he breathed a sigh of relief that as far as he could tell the coast was clear. Walking away from the depot and staying alert to what was going on around him, which appeared to be nothing unusual, he made his way to the outskirts of the city and up to Promontory Summit. He marveled at the notorious iron spike that marked the spot where the Union Pacific and the Central Pacific Railroads had joined three years earlier. It was the last spike driven into the ground marking the memorable meeting place of the two railroads.

"Wish I could have been here," he whispered. "I am sure it was a very auspicious day and time. Too bad the executives for Union Pacific were money hungry." Malachi stooped down and rubbed his hand over the golden spike feeling several indentions in it. Leaning forward, he took a closer look before voicing his thoughts. "It was reported that a Union Officer, four years after the close of the Civil

War, rode by and struck the spike with his sword. Wow, he would have had to hit it extremely hard over and over in the same spot to dent the iron. Maybe it is just a rumor, but if so, how *did* the marks get there?" Picking up his bag, he scanned up and down the rails before giving the golden spike another lingering look. "Yes, how perplexing that leading executives and high ranking government officials were that money hungry. Well, the Bible does state that 'the love of money is the root of all evil.'" After smoothing his hand once more over the spike, Malachi headed back toward Promontory City. He put his hand across his heart feeling the outline of the leather pouch beneath his shirt. "How utterly ridiculous that such a notorious occasion was marred by such greed. However, that is the reason I am here. If there had not been illegal acts involved, I may not have a job. For sure, not this one."

Chapter 17

Malachi entered a passenger car much smaller than the Union Pacific that had brought him from Colorado and across eastern Utah to Promontory. He eased onto the first available seat as the conductor shouted, "All aboard! Last call!" Leaving Promontory Summit and the golden spike behind did not erase the site from his memory. He pondered why someone could remain so full of hate to take a sword, four years after the conflict between the North and South had finally come to an end, and wham a golden iron spike so hard and so long until it would forever leave a mark.

The Utah Central Railway carried him southeast over the northern Promontory Mountains around winding curves and down steep grades, bypassing the Great Salt Lake. From a mountain top, he looked down at a surveyors camp located at the base of the mountain. Without binoculars he was barely able to detect the movement of two men who appeared as ants moving from mound to mound. His attention was drawn to several odd shaped buildings erected just beyond a mountain slope. The words Mine Mill were scrawled across the larger one and several tall pipes extending from one of the smaller buildings perked his interest. Windows of many sorts and sizes accented them all. Miners were relaxed against the side of a building much smaller than the others. In fact, from his point of view, it looked more like a minuscule hut.

Arriving in Salt Lake City, the train pulled into the small depot and came to a jolting stop. With bag in hand, Malachi stepped from a diminutive platform onto an unlevel, pitted, dirt road and headed to the point of his destination. Facing his new surroundings bravely, although not sure of what he may encounter, great relief washed over him when the dirt road became smoother and wider. Horse drawn carriage tracks were prevalent indicating he had entered the busy and prestigious area of the city. He was amazed at the great architectural structures which lined the busy thoroughfare. Coming to a stop in front of the most impressive building of all, he stepped from the main road onto a brick walk.

"This has to be it," he uttered, glancing around once more at the other buildings as if to reassure himself. "Yes. No doubt about it. This is the Governor's House." Continuing up the walk, he observed the detailed woodwork that adorned the posts and guard rails across the front of the porch and down one side. The bay and arched windows of the main house displayed more meticulous woodwork while gable and hip roofs gave it a unique appearance. He looked with admiration at a small room located in front center and appeared to be resting on top of the main dwelling. It's dome shaped roof added even more height and accented the architectural beauty of the building. Most impressive of all was the weather vane situated at the tip top of the dome with its graceful design, gently moving one way and then the other as a peaceful zephyr swept over the salt city.

Already running behind schedule, Malachi hurried up the steps of the building. Just as he reached the porch, the door of the Governor's House opened and two men stepped out. Although he had never seen him in person, Malachi recognized the Governor from pictures he had been privy to.

"Governor Woods?"

Both men looked at the young man before them. "Yes, I am Governor Woods."

"I have an appointment with you."

Neither man spoke. The Governor's companion gave Malachi a stern stare.

"I am Malachi Hebron. I'm sorry…"

The Governor's companion interrupted. "You are one hour and forty five minutes late."

"Yes sir. As I was saying, I am sorry to be late. The train had…" At another interruption, Malachi gave the man a bewildered look.

"Well, that is too bad. The Governor is on his way to a luncheon engagement. He cannot see you now."

Governor Woods held up his hand to silence the man. "Lunch can wait. Come on inside, Malachi."

"Yes sir." Malachi stepped onto the porch and stood beside the Governor.

When his companion opened his mouth to protest, Governor Woods held up his hand again. "It is okay. I want to see Malachi as much as he wants to see me." The Governor stepped through the entrance door with Malachi following close behind. Pausing just inside and looking back at his companion who was following them with a look of uncertainty, the Governor added, "Rather, I should say it is imperative that I speak with Malachi. You can wait in the lobby. This will not take long."

Malachi was now the one with a look of uncertainty as he followed the Governor into an immaculate room. He knew his mission for seeing Governor Woods was important, but the Governor delaying his luncheon and so emphatic about speaking with him brought a sense of urgency.

Governor Woods stood beside a mahogany desk that shined to perfection. Malachi's image was mirrored as he reached out to touch it but withdrew his hand quickly. The governor smiled. "You can touch it. It won't break. Feel free to sit if you want to, but as I said, this won't take long."

"I'll stand, Sir."

"I understand you are on a double assignment. Am I correct?"

"Yes sir."

"Again, correct me if I am wrong. A plot to assassinate President Grant has been uncovered. You were chosen to find out the names of the traitors or would be assassins and report back to D.C. before his reelection."

"Yes sir." Malachi reached inside his shirt and took out a leather pouch. "I have the names right here. This little leather pouch has survived the sabotage of the great ship, Onyx, the turbulent waves of the Ouachita and Boeuf Rivers, and the pursuit of outlaws over mountains and in lowlands. This leather pouch and I will make it all the way to the Capitol Building."

"You seem mighty sure of yourself."

"Oh not of myself, Governor Woods, but of Jesus Christ. To quote the Bible, 'For I can do all things through Christ which strengtheneth me.' You see, Jesus is the source of my strength. He is the Rock that keeps me safe. The Anchor that I hold to. I have been pursued by those who want not only the information in this pouch but would like to get rid of me for good. To be truthful, I must admit there have been moments of fear." Malachi chuckled. "More times than I can count I have felt like a gopher in a shallow hole. While fleeing from one place to another, at times barely escaping with my life and more than a little shaken, the Anchor held me steadfast. It will continue to do so as long as I stay attached to Him."

The Governor smiled. "Sounds like you are in good hands. Well, I am happy to tell you that I have no names to add to the list. Although Utah is not yet a part of the United States, it is considered United States Territory and President Grant appointed me as Governor. He is my friend. I have not and will not betray him. The man waiting outside is my top aide and he has proven his loyalty to me and the President. I trust him explicitly. Together we have combed this territory and have found nothing that points to anyone from Utah who is in on the plot."

"I am glad to hear that, Sir."

"Relating to the other matter, I have found nothing pointing to any of my constituents. As for my urgency to speak with you, you are to go from here to Washington DC and report directly to President Grant as fast as the Transcontinental Railroad can get you there. You must avoid any unnecessary stops along the way. Your orders have been changed."

"Changed?" Malachi asked. "How?"

"That I can't say. Your contact in Omaha has been notified. It was nice meeting you, Malachi, but you have more important things to do. So, you had better be on your way. You be very cautious. Those who are involved in this treason know when the information you carry reaches the President, as the saying goes, heads will roll. Considering what you have already experienced, you are an open target."

"Thank you, Sir, but that goes with the territory."

Chapter 18

Staring out the window of the train that was carrying him across Utah Territory, Malachi wondered what this day held for him. Not having an inkling as to why his orders had been changed but using past meetings as a precedent, he was sure that his urgent return to Washington D.C. was of utmost necessity. He closed his eyes and tried to relax. The swerving car followed the twists and turns and ups and downs of the rails carrying him back through the Rocky Mountains of Colorado. The longing in his heart to return to Dotson Farm was almost unbearable. Nevertheless, to disobey orders would not be wise. Deborah and her safety filled his days and sleepless nights while the train rumbled on carrying him east on what seemed to be an endless journey.

As the tracks stretched around and over the great Smokies, sometimes dangerously close to the edge of steep cliffs and over high mountain peaks, his thoughts went to Gideon and Abigail and their thriving ranch near Tollesboro, Kentucky. He would have loved to confide some of his experiences and fears to Gideon, who next to Papa, was his role model. Thoughts of Papa and Momma and Bethel surfaced to the forefront of his mind. *Bethel is a place of healing. A safe place. Safety is definitely not what I am feeling at this moment.* The words of Governor Woods weighed heavily on his mind. *Considering what you have already experienced, you are an open target.* He sat erect and looked around him with a sudden instinct that maybe even now, at this very moment, the Governor's words were a reality.

Weary from the seven day train ride from Salt Lake City and trying to get a grip on his nerves, he turned back to the window as the Transcontinental Rails carried him along the Potomac River, past the Washington Monument located on the National Mall and towering over Washington D.C. The colossal obelisk which never ceased to inspire him was built in honor of the great Founding Father of this country, George Washington. Tilting his head, he endeavored to get a glimpse of the very top as it tapered to a hollow shaft rising to a maximum of 555 feet and appearing much smaller than the actual size of the massive structure. "Wow," he whispered.

The train gradually slowed its speed and pulled into the depot at D.C. Malachi stood, stretched his stiff legs and muscles and removed his bag from the cubbyhole above his head. Out of sheer habit and caution, he took another look around the passenger car. Taking his place in the aisle while enduring a few bumps from other weary passengers, he soon made his exit. Lingering on the platform of the depot, he took a deep breath hoping to inhale some fresh air but was rudely rewarded with the stagnant smell of the Capital City. While efforts had been made to improve the situation, a foul smell still drifted in from the polluted Potomac. The words of Governor Woods kept nagging at his brain. *An open target. An open target.*

Anxiously scanning the area and being as inconspicuous as possible, he spied a shadow a short distance from the platform. Knowing it could be from most anything and about to dismiss it and be on his way, a movement arrested him. The shadow suddenly took on the form of a man, who at that moment, was headed his direction. Apparently he had second thoughts, for he stopped and leaned against the side of a building intentionally adverting his eyes away from the depot. The dark suit, dark glasses and hat titled slightly forward offered a man of importance, but Malachi knew it could just as easily be a disguise. Forgetting about the polluted air, he spotted a cabbie waiting nearby. Wanting to run to it yet not wanting to arouse suspicion in case the man was out to thwart his mission, nonchalantly, he made his way to the cabbie. "Take me to the

Capitol." He and the cabbie took their places inside the carriage. "Make it as quickly as possible, please."

As the cabbie took hold of the harness lines of the team, Malachi continued to look back with searching eyes for any sign that he was being followed. The well-dressed man he had spotted some distance from the station was now standing on the depot platform. To his disappointment, Malachi barely got a glimpse of the man before he disappeared among all the others who had chosen to get their daily exercise by walking along the busy main road of the Capital City.

"Just my luck," Malachi uttered. "Oh, well, if he is trailing me, I will know it sooner or later."

The cabbie paid no attention to Malachi but kept focused on the task of getting him to the Capitol. As he weaved back and forth dodging pedestrians who refused to yield any space, and other carriages that claimed the right of way, the cabbie managed to keep control of the team. He stayed calm and claimed his territory while Malachi held his breath holding onto the edge of the carriage at each close call.

Realizing he had better do something before he keeled over and maybe even fall out of the carriage, he released a long held breath. "Whew." Mumbling, he wiped the perspiration beads from his brow. "Cabbie, you are as cool as a cucumber, while I am sweating like morning dew."

"No worry. I'll get you there."

"Yeah, but what condition will I be in when you do. I hope all in one piece. I have a meeting with the President."

"The President, huh? Well, this is not my first trip down this busy street. Had lots of practice. You will still be all in one piece, I promise. Relax."

Malachi took several deep breaths. *I'm not sure how reliable his promise is. Relax, he says. May as well try.*

The ten minute ride from the depot had seemed more like thirty when the cabbie finally pulled the team to a stop in front of the iron gate that opened to the grounds of the Capitol. Malachi paid the driver, picked up his bag and stepped from the carriage. Pausing outside the gate, he passed his identification card through the bars to a soldier holding a rifle. The soldier looked at the card, then back at him. With a stern stare, he appeared to be studying Malachi then gradually turned his attention back to the card. It was obvious the soldier was not in a hurry to admit him onto the grounds. Malachi's insides were screaming, *I am who that says I am. Just open the gate, please.* He stared at the soldier while endeavoring to retain his patience. Without a word, the soldier returned the card and stepped aside as the gate swung open.

Malachi walked with haste toward the Capitol. About half way up a brick walk, he came to an abrupt halt and stared upward. He gazed with wonder at the crowning feature of the Dome resting atop the United States Capitol Building, the Statue of Freedom. He saw a very modestly dressed female figure with long, flowing hair. On the top of her head was a helmet with a crest composed of an eagle's head and feathers. A brooch with the inscription "U S" adorned the top of the dress. Draped over it was a heavy, flowing toga fringed with fur and decorative balls. Taking a few more steps with eyes still glued on the Statue of Freedom, he found it very interesting that the right hand of the lady rested upon the top of a sheathed sword that was wrapped in a scarf. In her left hand was a laurel wreath of victory and the shield of the United States with thirteen stripes. Malachi slowly let his gaze move downward and saw the lady was attached to a cast iron pedestal topped with a globe and encircled with a motto. Slowly and distinctly, he read, "E Pluribus Unum. And that, Malachi, means, 'Out of many, one.'" He chuckled. "There was a time when I didn't know the English meaning of those Latin words."

Still unable to force himself to get on with the important business and new orders that awaited him, he looked upward again at the crest of Freedom's headdress rising an amazing 288 feet above the East Front Plaza. He gazed in wonder at the nine stars that encircled the headcovering of the Statue. Beholding the awesome masterpiece that stood tall and erect before him, Malachi was moved beyond words. He knew the helmet, itself, represented the fact that some of the people who worked to create the great Statue of Freedom were not free themselves.

He stood transfixed until his own voice, although barely above a whisper, broke in on the solemn moment. "The most astounding thing of the whole artistic sculpture is the fact the artist chose a woman to represent freedom and placed the amazing eagle upon the helmet covering her head." Another hushed stillness settled upon him. Then in a trembling voice he uttered, "I sincerely believe the real reason is because many, many years before there ever was a United States of America, a woman was chosen by the Almighty God to birth the One who would bring freedom throughout the ages to an enslaved world. Jesus did proclaim in Luke 4:18, He was sent 'to preach deliverance to the captive…to set at liberty them that are bruised.'"

So engrossed in the magnificent sculpture and his sudden inspiring revelation of what the Statue of Freedom represented, he was not even aware someone had approached until a quiet demanding voice interrupted his most gripping moment.

"Young man, no loitering is allowed on the Capitol grounds."

Surprised, Malachi slowly turned and stared into the faces of two armed guards standing within an arm's reach and holding rifles to attention. Without hesitation he walked away, giving only a backward glance. To his relief the guards were not following, however, their eyes remained glued steadfast on him until he walked up the steps of the building. After going through the necessary scrutiny of security, he stepped inside the Capitol.

"Wow! Not taking any chances now, are they?" He said to the guard who opened the door.

The guard's only response was nothing more than a forward head nod. Malachi followed behind but still proceeded to make conversation. "I suppose, though, it is a good and necessary precaution since the assassination of President Lincoln and considering the rumor…"

The guard stopped, turned and gave him a provoking stare. Malachi swallowed the lump in his throat with a gulp. Silently, he followed the guard up a flight of stairs to the second floor and into a room of rare grandeur. The guard did not hesitate, but Malachi stopped in the center of the room and looked upward through a large circular opening. He was captivated by the painting that could be seen on the ceiling of the oculus. He jumped when he felt the butt of a rifle in his ribs.

"Ooops. I'm sorry. I do get carried away sometimes."

The guard gave him a sideways look and another forward head nod.

"The painting is amazing." Malachi chuckled. "Except I don't care much for the gods and goddesses the painter depicted in it. However, I am thankful for the memory portrayed of George Washington and the American Heroes that adorns the ceiling of the Dome."

The guard stopped again, giving him an intimidating look. "You talk too much. The fresco painting is known as the Apotheosis of Washington. Now, please keep your mouth closed and follow me."

Malachi returned his look stare to stare. *You will not intimidate me.* However, he thought it best to obey the guard. After all, the man did have the advantage. Attributing his excessive talking to anxiousness about what lay ahead of him, he fell in step, slightly behind and to the side of the guard.

Chapter 19

Leaving the Capitol grounds and escorted by two guards who had received direct orders from President Grant to ensure his safety to the train depot, Malachi relaxed in the seat of the President's illustrious carriage. Thankful for the reprieve of having to always be on the alert and looking over his shoulder for suspicious characters, he closed his eyes and allowed visions of Deborah to completely take control. Remembering the first time he saw her, that same feeling of love at first sight washed over him. He knew after seeing her, there would never be another girl for him. He had visions of them riding across the plantation the times she had visited Bethel. All the family had immediately fallen in love with her. Recalling Momma's words, a smile creased his countenance. *You two are a good match and obviously very much in love. Don't rush into anything. You are both so very young. You do not always have to seize the moment. Some things are very pertinent and can't wait, but true love is enduring. It is patient.*

Remembering his reply only made him more anxious to complete this assignment so they could be together. *Don't worry, Momma, I am not about to get married any time soon. Neither of us are ready. Deborah reminds me of you. I look at her and see goodness. She is so transparent. It is almost like I can see into her very soul.* He smiled at the memory of their first kiss. *It was only a peck on the cheek while we were standing near the train depot in Pueblo, Colorado.* He recalled the feel of her hand in his. *It was so soft. I squeezed it and she looked at me with dark, sparkling eyes and whispered, I love you, Malachi.*

"I love you, Deborah Dotson. When will I see you again? I wanted to let you know about my change of orders but there wasn't time." So caught up in his meditations, he did not even realize his voice was audible. Had he opened his eyes, he would have seen two usually solemn guards looking at him and smiling. Thoughts of the Dotson dairy brought afresh the night he was tracked to the farm. Remembering how he outwitted his pursuer by letting Articus out of the pen, he released a chuckle. Aroused by his own laughter, he opened his eyes and the reality of his future struck with full force.

The protected ride from the Capitol ended as soon as Malachi stepped from the Presidential carriage onto the platform of the depot. On his own, again, he glanced around remembering the man who had stepped from the shadows into his view that morning. Not seeing anyone who resembled the man, he boarded the train, found a seat half way down the aisle and tried to erase the image from his mind. Relaxing was out of the question, knowing he must stay alert and cautious. He was on his own. With trepidation he recalled the parting words of President Grant. *Malachi, you are no longer considered just a government agent. You are now a Diplomatic Courier. You will be walking on thin ice. Walk very lightly. Maybe even tiptoe. Always remember, the important thing is what a man is, not what he seems.*

Muttering, so as not to be understood by other passengers, Malachi smoothed his right hand over the boxed shaped metal item that rested on his lap. "Well, little attaché case, you and I are bound together it seems." Slipping his hand under the sleeve of his jacket, he touched a metal ring that was partially covered by his shirt sleeve and attached to his wrist. Touching the handle and two metal locks of the case, he looked about before continuing in a subdued verbal dialogue. "Yep, we are linked together by this little thing. You are quite different from the original one that was invented in 1826. From what I've been told, it was nothing more than an iron frame with a carpet covering. But it is not you that is important. It's what is inside you."

His own words, although nothing more than barely a whisper, brought a hushed silence to him as further warnings from the President gripped him. *The person you come in contact with may not really be on the inside what he appears to be on the outside. You will do well to remember the contents of a package is not determined by its outward appearance. It may be wrapped in pretty paper and adorned with lavish bows, but that doesn't mean there is something beautiful and harmless under the covering. You have to pull off the bows and tear away the wrappings to see what is concealed on the inside. So Malachi, before you release any vital information, go beyond what you see on the outside, pull off the packaging and take a good inward look.*

His cogitations were interrupted when a man sauntered down the aisle and bumped into him. Malachi wasn't sure if it was accidental or on purpose until the man leaned over and reached for the attaché case. All doubts of being accidental fled his mind. Without flinching a muscle, he stared at the man and slowly pushed up his coat sleeve.

The man, momentarily, let his eyes rest on the iron cuff before straightening himself to a standing position. "Uh, I beg your pardon. That case isn't going anywhere."

Staring the man down, Malachi replied. "No, not unless you drag me with it. If I were you, I would not attempt to do so."

"Allow me to sit with you."

Before Malachi could reply, the man turned as a commanding voice behind him said, "No. That is my seat. Go sit somewhere else."

The man tipped his hat and without another word sauntered on down the aisle.

Malachi kept his eyes glued on the owner of the voice. He smiled at an elderly lady wearing large spectacles, with one hand resting on a walking stick and clutching a rather large reticule under her other arm. She dropped her reticule in the aisle beside him. Reaching down to pick it up, he quickly withdrew his hand when she whammed it with her walking stick. His smile turned to a look of curious bewilderment.

"Mind your own business, young fellah." She was about to loop her stick through the handle of her reticule when the gentleman next in line bent over to pick it up. He straightened up quickly when he got a wallow across the arm. "You, too." Not caring there were several people standing in the aisle waiting to take their seats, she proceeded to pick up the reticule with her stick and plopped it down near Malachi's feet. "Scoot over, Sonny, so I can sit here."

Obediently, Malachi moved over next to the window. He found the old lady quite humorous but was afraid even to smile, lest he get another wham with the walking stick. He attempted to ignore her staring at the attaché case until with the crook of her stick, she pulled up his coat sleeve.

"What you got thar, Sonny?"

Malachi smiled. Before he could speak, she said, "Must be something mighty important to be 'tached to you like that."

"It is."

She looked over the rim of her spectacles. "Not very talkative are you, Sonny? Well, I admit I'm a bit nosey. Just a busybody, as some folks say, but…"

The train whistle drowned out her voice letting Malachi know they would soon be leaving the depot. He tried to get comfortable and closed his eyes, hoping that would quieten his nosey companion.

"Huh," she uttered.

Deciding to take a peek at her, in a squint-eyed manner he attempted a look with his left eye. She was still staring at the attaché case. Knowing he need not worry, at least not at present, with a smile, he closed his eye. Only a few minutes had passed when he heard a noise beside him. Opening both eyes, he put his hand over his mouth to force back the chuckle that threatened to erupt. The old woman had her head reared back, mouth open and was snoring so loudly she had the attention of half the train.

Nearly two days passed before Malachi reached his destination. The conductor's booming voice brought all passengers to their feet. "Everyone off. This is as far as this train goes."

Malachi considered helping the old lady, but on second thought decided against it, preferring to avoid another whack on his hand.

Pointing the walking stick at her reticule, she said, "Be a gentleman, Sonny, and carry that thing for me."

With the reticule under his arm, his own bag in his right hand and the attaché case in his left, he followed her off the train.

The old woman looked at him over the rim of her spectacles, giving him a slight poke in the chest with her stick. "Sonny, don't be a fool. Some people wear a disguise. They are not always what they seem to be." Before he could utter a word, she snatched the reticule from under his arm and ambled away from the depot, leaning on her walking stick.

Malachi watched her. The Presidents warning flashed through his mind. *People are not always what they seem to be. That's strange. She told me the same thing. Hmm. Is she really an old lady? I wonder. Does she really need those spectacles and walking stick?* Walking away from the depot, he turned around to see if she was still in sight. He caught a glimpse of her backside as she hobbled her way through the mingling crowd. "Malachi Hebron, now you are suspecting old ladies." Dismissing the thought that maybe she was not what she seemed to be, with determination he walked toward a nearby cabbie.

Chapter 20

Deborah stood near a guard rail on the deck of the SS Atlantic. The great ocean liner was still at rest in New York Harbor nestled on a narrow strip of water close to Staten Island. Staring out across the water, she welcomed the breeze that drifted in from the Atlantic Ocean and relished the solitude of the relaxing zephyr. Lost in the beauty of the glistening waters of the Atlantic, she wiped away strains of hair that blew across her face obscuring her vision. Awareness of other passengers aboard the ship were nil until the noise of a loud cacophony caused her to turn. She grabbed hold of the guard rail just in the nick of time. Otherwise, she would have been splattered on the deck floor by a lad who whammed carelessly into her. Before she could catch her breath, he skedaddled away leaving all those nearby in a frenzy.

"You come back here, you little scoundrel!" A deck hand screamed as he ran past Deborah, hot in pursuit of the small boy. However, he was no match for the nimble lad who never looked back but kept running lickety split as fast as possible weaving in and out among passengers. She watched in awe as some reached out to grab hold of the small waif, but he always managed to escape their grip.

After that little incident and deciding it probably would be to her advantage to pay more attention to the other passengers, she mingled around on deck knowing the SS Atlantic was known for its safety and comfort. It was made famous by carrying high style and the society of the day. Vacationers, and others from not so prestigious backgrounds, mixed with the rich and renowned. In Deborah's eyes one was the same as another. To her, the so called elite was of no more importance than the least among society. Ladies were sporting umbrellas with arms looped through that of gentlemen wearing top hats, expensive clothing and sporting canes in which to ward off such as the small urchin that had all but knocked her down. Her eyes came to rest upon a young man and woman with an infant in her arms and a small girl clinging to her dress. Sizing up the crowd aboard the ocean liner, Deborah recalled the words of Mawmaw Dorcas. *One is not rich by earthly possessions but by purity and goodness of conscience and heart. That is the only true wealth.*

Captivated by the hustle and bustle of passengers moving about, each absorbed in his own little world, she recalled a portion of the poem by Ella Wheeler Wilcox. Walking back toward the guard rail and so struck by the poetic words that seemed to fit the moment, she voiced them.

> "Not the happy and sad, for the swift flying years,
> Bring each man his laughter, each man his tears.
> Not the rich and the poor, for to rate a man's wealth,
> You must know the state of his conscience and health.
> Not the humble and proud, for in life's little span,
> Who puts on vain airs is not counted a man."

Deborah was surprised when a man stopped beside her. "Were you speaking to me, Mam?"

Startled, Deborah looked up at him. "Oh, no. Just voicing my thoughts."

When the man lingered attempting to make conversation, suspicion and wariness arrested her. Words that were drilled into her as a government agent in training, now were like a hammer pounding in her brain. *Trust no one. Trust no one.*

"Are you traveling alone? If so, allow me the honor."

Trust no one. "Excuse me, please." Deborah replied then turned and walked away. She dared not turn around but could feel his eyes boring into her back. Had she risked a backward glance, she would have discovered that to be true and would have also detected the smirky grin of interest that covered his countenance. She forced her eyes to look forward, trying to maintain a nonchalant walk. Mingling among the other passengers while endeavoring to hide from his view, words kept going over and over in her mind. *Wonder who he is? Wonder what he knows? Trust no one. Trust no one.*

She stopped dead still where she was, unaware that other passengers were having to step aside to keep from bumping into her. Becoming conscious of weird and hostile looks coming her way like darts, made her even more distrustful. *This is not good. Deborah you are becoming very paranoiac.* Taking a few steps and trying to be less conspicuous, thoughts bombarded her. *Trust no one. I am supposed to meet a contact here. If I trust no one, how will I know when we meet? This is not like meeting at Dorsey's Store in Pueblo. This is a strange place. Strange people. I have never been on an ocean liner before, much less about to sail across the Atlantic Ocean.* Making her way through the mass of people to the deck railing, she glanced about but saw no sign of the man who was too interested in her and had brought uneasiness to her once peaceful solitude.

"I don't see him, but that doesn't mean he can't see me," she whispered. Looking out over the ocean again, her attempt to reclaim the tranquility she had felt before the interruption, failed. Placidity refused to surface. "Maybe he is my contact. No. He made me uncomfortable. Almost afraid." She strolled along the railing continuing the dialogue with herself. "Being afraid is no good indication that the man was up to mischief. Being afraid goes with the job." Suddenly, she felt as if there were thousands of eyes boring holes in her. Glancing around, she realized how near to the truth that was. People were staring at her. Some even walked past and then glanced back for another look. "What are they staring at?" She questioned. "Oh!" Covering her mouth to prevent a laugh out loud, she realized her voice had changed from a mere whisper to a near shout.

Gathering her wits about her, Deborah tried to bring her thoughts and emotions under control. While emotions seemed easy to conquer, her thoughts did not. *Maybe I should wander around and try to locate my contact. No. I was told to wait on the middle deck. The contact will find me and will identify himself by using the passcode.* As she gazed again across the massive ocean, the appearance of variations of colors, from sky blue to navy to violet hues, amazed her but did not disrupt her thoughts. Taking a small pendant watch from her reticule, she released a heavy sigh. "I surely wish my contact would make himself known. This ship is due to pull out of harbor in thirty minutes."

She jumped at the not too gentle touch of a hand on her arm. "So we meet again."

"Oh!" Deborah looked up into the eyes of the man who had approached her earlier. She removed his hand. "You startled me."

"I seem to be good at that. Approaching you by surprise, I mean. I beg your forgiveness."

Deborah looked at him. *Trust no one. Trust no one.* She didn't speak.

"Well, I guess I am not forgiven. Let's see. What can I do to have the pleasure of your company for a while?"

Deborah gave him an unflinching stare but still did not speak.

He looked at her, curiously. "So, are you ready to talk to me. Tell me your name. Are you vacationing? If so, where are you going? I may want to go along."

Further warnings from her superiors jumped to the forefront of her mind. *Do not, under any circumstance, give the slightest hint in word or action that you are on government business. Wait for the passcode.* Sick and tired of him and his egotistical attitude, Deborah demanded,

"Mister, you are making a nuisance of yourself. If you are aching for company, go find someone else and leave me alone."

"But I am not interested in anyone else. Let's you and I find a more private place to get acquainted." He placed a tight grip on her arm.

Deborah tried to remove his hand, but he held it rigidly.

"Remove your hand from my arm." She spoke firmly and with a courage she did not feel.

"But we have some things to discuss. Can't do it here." He held her fast and gave her arm a jerk.

"I said let go of me!"

"No, my dear. You are coming with me." He put his arm tightly around her waist.

"Remove your arm. We are already drawing attention. Do it now or I will make a spectacle of you. I will have you removed from this ship…"

She was interrupted as a young man stepped in front of her. "Is this rogue bothering you, sweetheart?" He looked at the obnoxious man. "Remove your arm. I could do it for you, but I had rather use my energy in a more beneficial way." With those words, he gave the rogue a hard punch in the face which landed him flat of his back and sprawled out on the deck floor. "Now," the young man said and looked at Deborah. "For the more important things." He kissed her before she could utter a word.

Chapter 21

Astounded, Deborah looked wide-eyed at the man who saved her moment but also had taken his liberty to kiss her. "Malachi," she whispered. "At first I thought I was hallucinating. That is, until you kissed me. Did you come to New York just to see me off? How did you know I would be on the SS Atlantic?" She noticed the attaché case but thought nothing of it having seen him carrying similar cases before.

Putting his arm around her, Malachi glanced downward. At his feet lay a folded piece of paper. He picked it up. "Wonder where this came from?"

Deborah watched quietly as he unfolded the paper. He made no effort to read it aloud, but stared into the distance as if unaware she was there. She put her hand on his arm. "What is it, Malachi? What is in the note?"

Malachi gazed around the deck of the ship as if searching for someone. He crumpled the note in his hand and attempted to cram it into his pocket.

Deborah grabbed hold of his hand. "What is in the note, Malachi?"

He looked at her. "It's not necessarily what is in the note."

"Well, what is it, then?"

He hung his head. "It is you, Deb."

"Me? I...I don't understand." Taking the piece of paper from his hand, mumbling, she voiced the words. "Remember, you two are not supposed to know each other." She opened her mouth but no words came. Surprised, but relieved, she stared at him with mouth agape. Neither spoke. Finally, in a squeaky voice, she uttered, "You? You are my contact, Malachi?"

Refusing to look into her face, he turned and took a few steps, leaving her staring at his back.

Deborah glared at him. She stood where she was, fighting back tears. After allowing him some time to get control of his own emotions, which was exactly what he was trying to do, she walked up to where he stood, leaving a distance between them but close enough so they could hear each other speak. "I didn't know. They needed a female agent to go to Paris and be a part of an important assignment. They needed someone who could be discreet and yet bold at the same time. I was chosen." When Malachi didn't speak, she continued. "Although limited, I can speak and understand the French language which helped them to make their choice. I don't even know what I am supposed to do, really. I was told my contact is in charge of this assignment and would brief me on my duties. Furthermore, I was willing and excited about going to Paris, France."

"Willing and excited? Had this been a pleasure trip, maybe so. But even that would be risky. There is so much unrest in France, now." He paused. "This is a dangerous assignment, Deb. It wasn't fair for headquarters to not make you aware of that."

"They told me it could be risky."

"Risky? That is putting it mildly. There is still time for you to refuse. The ship is still docked in Harbor Bay. Go to D.C. and let them know."

"I can't do that, Malachi. I have already been briefed on some things."

"By the way, when were you in D. C.?"

"Five days ago. Guess we missed each other by a few days."

"Headquarters planned it that way. For security purposes, they don't want their secret agents who are working together to be there at the same time."

"It will be fun. We will be traveling together across the wide Atlantic Ocean."

Malachi looked at her, forcing himself to keep his distance. "Fun? I love you, Deb. We will be traveling on the same ship for days and are not supposed to even know one another. That is not possible."

"We can get together sometime and somewhere. We do have to communicate."

"Pretending to meet accidentally in the dining area, or on the deck? What fun is that?" He pulled up his shirt sleeve revealing the handcuff on his arm.

Deborah opened her mouth in astonishment. She managed to eke out a few words. "The case. It's…it is attached to your arm."

"Walk away, quickly, Deb," he uttered. "We are being watched. Act as if you are very angry at me. If that is possible." He grinned. "I will meet you back on deck later. Hurry. Now."

Malachi bowed as she walked away so as to convince onlookers they were complete strangers. Staying where he was until seeing a man lurking near a support column of the ship, very nonchalantly he headed in that direction. Recognizing the man as the one he had sent sprawling to the deck floor, he quickened his pace. Giving a cautious backward glance, he spied Deborah standing against the deck rail. Resisting the urge to rush back to her, he hastened forward with the intention of approaching the man near the column. To his chagrin the man had disappeared. With searching eyes, Malachi roved around the deck but saw no sign of him. *Hmm, seems as if he disappeared into thin air.* Torn between what he wanted to do, which was to be with Deborah, or to obey orders and treat her as a stranger, tugged at his mind. A bit disgruntled about the whole situation, he cast one more look in her direction, then pulled a ticket stub from his shirt pocket. *Stateroom 312. May as well check it out.*

"I can say this for the government, they do things first class when it comes to accommodations," he uttered, looking around the room. "Can't say that is true about their political involvements. At least some of them." Anxiously, he walked back and forth from one side of the room to the other. "That is why you are sailing across the ocean. To separate the good from the bad. The sheep from the goats. That's the Bible definition." Continuing to pace around the room, he paused for a look through the porthole. *Wonder when this ship is going to leave harbor?* Nervously, he piddled with the handcuff around his arm. *I'll be glad to get rid of this thing. It's as troublesome as if I had a millstone hanging around my neck.* With an effort to calm the restlessness that possessed him, he threw himself across the bed. However, rest evaded him completely. He sat up and flung his legs over the side of the mattress. *I must check on Deb.* Like a bolt of lightning it struck him. *What if that man found her. What if he forced her to go with him.* In a flash, he was at the stateroom door. Being sure he had his pistol and that it was well concealed, he stepped into the narrow hallway. *Maybe we are supposed to be strangers, but I am still responsible for her safety. Afterall, she is my assistant. Although, that fact cannot be known.*

Quickly he made his way to the middle deck which was still crowded with passengers. Weaving in and out among idlers, he maneuvered his way to the deck railing. Scanning it from one end to the other, his heart skipped a beat when he did not see her. Forgetting about being passive, with searching eyes he hurried amidst the crowd. *Where is she? Maybe she went to her stateroom. I didn't even ask for the number. No. I told her we would meet back on deck. She would be here unless...*Fast approaching the panic stage, he refused to let disturbing thoughts take over his sanity. Pushing his way through the throng of passengers who were still lollygagging around the deck, he headed back to the railing. Once again, his eyes went from one end of it to the other, but Deborah was nowhere in sight. He leaned against it and stared out over the ocean, pondering what to do.

"Guess I can go to the staterooms and knock on every door until I find her," he uttered. "But that may not set too well with those who cherish their privacy." Miserable and no longer able to remain idle, he was about to return to his room when Deborah stepped from a group of people and walked to the railing some distance from where he stood. Trying not to attract attention, he meandered his way toward her. To his chagrin, other passengers stopped beside her taking up the empty spaces. *Just my luck.* Nevertheless, boldly, he approached her. "So we meet again, Mam." He tipped his hat and squeezed in between her and a middle aged man.

The man gave Malachi a 'get lost' look then focused his eyes on Deborah. "Is this man bothering you? If so, I can take care of him."

Deborah smiled. "It's okay." She looked at Malachi. "May as well give him the pleasure of my company for a while, but he can keep his kisses to himself."

"Thank you, kindly, Mam. I'm not so bad. Shall we find a place that is less crowded? You may even decide to like me." With Malachi's hand on her elbow, they walked away from the railing. Turning his head slightly, out of the corner of his eye he saw the man staring at the attaché case. However, at the moment he was only interested in Deborah. "You are taking it seriously, aren't you?"

"What?"

"The orders that we are not supposed to know each other."

"Yes. Don't you?"

"Only because I have to. I surely don't want to. It is so hard." He stopped walking. "I have a great idea."

Deborah stopped beside him. "Oh?"

"Let's get married in Paris."

"Mala…!" Noticing several people staring at her in passing, she clamped her hand over her mouth realizing her voice was louder than normal. Covering her mistake quickly, she said, "Mind your own business."

"You are my business," he whispered.

Lowering her tone so only he could hear, she replied, "Oh Malachi, we have a job to do. Let's make the most of it. We may never work together again. By the way, you have not given me the passcode."

Although wanting to put his arm around her, he knew just a touch would have to suffice for the moment. "Look at me. I love you, Deborah Dotson."

"That is not the passcode. Wonder when we are going to leave Harbor Bay?"

"Prospects are good. The ship seems to be moving. Deb, you know me, and I know you so why use the passcode?"

"Because we must obey orders. What is the passcode? Malachi, say it." At that instant, the blast of a horn vibrated through the atmosphere startling Deborah and drowning out their voices.

Chapter 22

Malachi stepped from his stateroom closing the door quietly behind him. The attaché case was secured to his arm as he made his way down the narrow hall and took a flight of steps up to the fourth deck. With trepidation, yet with great anticipation, he walked past the bridge of the ship straight to a door with a metal sign across the front. After taking a deep breath, he uttered the words that were etched into the metal. "Private. Captain's Quarters." Summoned there by the note that was slipped under his stateroom door, he was surprised considering the fact he and the Captain had never met. Puzzled and hesitating before knocking, he analyzed the situation. *What could the Captain want with me? The greater mystery is who delivered the note. This is the second one. Someone on this ship, other than Deb, knows me.* Feeling a prickling of dread, he shuttered at the unwelcome thoughts that were trying to find a lodging place in his brain.

"What are you doing on this deck, young man?"

Startled, Malachi turned and stared at a man standing about three feet behind him with a Deputy Captain label on his shirt. Feeling like a frog had lodged in his throat, he swallowed with a big gulp. Before he could speak, two men appeared seemingly out of nowhere and strong arms grabbed him under his elbows lifting him off his feet. Malachi kept turning his head from one side to the other looking at his abductors, who refused to let him walk alone. Stunned at what was happening, he held his peace while noticing that one of the men kept his head slightly averted and turned his face completely away when Malachi looked his direction. With his feet in midair, the two men carried him to the bridge of the ship. Depositing him abruptly, Malachi staggered when his feet hit the floor.

The Deputy Captain dismissed the shipmates then turned his attention to Malachi. "I repeat, what are you doing on this deck?"

Malachi watched the men walk away. There was something familiar about one of them. So engrossed in thought and who the man could be, he did not respond to the deputy but kept staring intensely at the man's back. Pondering on what had just happened to him, he pointed a wobbly finger at the retreating man. "I...I think I have seen one of them before. The one on the..."

The Deputy Captain interrupted. "I doubt it. Forget about him. It is not important. What were you doing standing outside the Captain's door?"

Malachi dared not voice his thoughts. *It's important to me.* He continued to watch the retreating man until he disappeared.

"Again I ask, what were you doing standing outside the Captain's door? Must I repeat everything I say?"

"I'm sorry, sir." Malachi put his hand on the attaché case. "I am a Diplomatic Courier for the American Government."

"You are, huh? I am not that easily convinced." He scrutinized the case and flippantly touched the handcuff on Malachi's arm. "This could be stolen."

Malachi glared at the man in disbelief. Refusing to be intimidated, he spoke as boldly as he dared endeavoring not to be disrespectful. Afterall, the man was an officer. "I was summoned to join the Captain in his stateroom."

"Really? By whom?"

"I don't know by whom. This note was slipped under the door of my room."

The officer accepted the note. After reading the summons, he looked at the attaché case then at Malachi. "Very well. The next time you come to this deck, you would do well to stop by the bridge first and let me or the officer on duty know what you are up to. It matters none whatsoever as to what you call yourself or who sent you. Come with me."

Malachi obeyed and stood silently as the officer knocked on the door. He was surprised when it opened promptly, and the ship's Captain stood before him.

"Captain, this man was summoned to your stateroom by this note that was slipped under his door. He does not know the bearer of it."

Accepting the note, the Captain didn't bother to read it. "Oh, yes." He scrutinized Malachi then moved aside, clearing the doorway.

After allowing Malachi to enter, the Captain stepped outside the room leaving the door ajar. The fact that he and the deputy exchanged whispers, only added to Malachi's bewilderment as to what was really going on. He waited. Barely able to tolerate the suspense, he was chomping at the bit. *If I ease a little closer to the door, maybe I can catch a word or two.* Before he could act upon that thought, the Captain entered the room and closed the door. "I am Captain Johns. Captain of this ocean liner makes me the most important man on the SS Atlantic. With it comes a huge responsibility. When I accepted the job and title as Captain, I also accepted the responsibility. Sit down, Malachi."

"You know my name, Sir? You know who I am?"

"That is just one part of my responsibilities. I check the names of passengers sailing on this ship. All are supposed to write down their occupation and if they are on a business or pleasure trip. Sorry to say, some have not always been truthful. The very elite of society sails on the SS Atlantic, along with the less well to do."

"Then you know why I am on the SS Atlantic?"

"I know quite a bit about you, Malachi Hebron. I know for some time you were a Government Agent and are now on your first assignment as a Diplomatic Courier. I know, also, what you have in that case attached to your arm is of vital importance."

"You know what is in here?" Malachi touched the attaché case.

"No. I do not know what your mission is. I do know that as a Diplomatic Courier, your protection and whatever is in that case is top priority."

Baffled and speechless, Malachi stared at Captain Johns. With that assurance, he didn't know whether to feel more confident of accomplishing his mission, or if he felt more threatened of an interference that would abort it. Happenings of the past few days flashed through his mind. *The man at the train depot in Washington D.C. The little old lady on the train, and the man he knocked flat to the deck floor of this ocean liner.*

He thought of Deborah. Concern for her safety was pressing on him. "Captain Johns, what if I have an assistant on this ship? Would that person be top priority, too?"

"No. That one will be your responsibility. I only promised to give you protection. Hopefully, I can do that. I understand you have already run into a bit of trouble over some young woman."

"Yes sir."

"Obviously, you can do a pretty good job of taking care of an assistant, should the need arise. Well, I must get back to my duties. Just wanted to let you know every effort will be made to protect you. Whether you benefit from that protection, at times, may depend entirely upon you. Even if it means jumping into the Atlantic Ocean." Captain Johns opened the door as a sign for Malachi to leave. "You appear to be solid and reliable. I am sure you are trustworthy or you would not have been chosen for the job. There are still several days before we reach the coast of France. Anything could happen. Stay alert and cautious. Prove you are worthy of the confidence attributed to you."

"Yes sir. I will do my best."

"Sometimes, not to disillusion you, but sometimes our best is not enough."

"I have always believed if you do your best, that is all you can do."

"No. That is not all you can do."

"But if I do my best and fail, what else is there?"

Captain Johns shook his hand. "You try again, Malachi."

Chapter 23

Deborah shrank into the shadow of a supporting post on the middle deck. The sailing lights of the ocean liner reflecting on small areas cast forth a dim glow. Definitely, it was not sufficient light for a young woman to be wandering around on deck at night. Even so, she pushed aside the urge to hurry back to her safe quarters. Surprised by a sound, she held her breath being silent and still as a mouse. All was quiet. Slowly exhaling, she moved closer to the support post. *What if security saw me sneaking from my room?* A more frighting thought struct her. *Worse still, what if the man who tried to force me to go with him the day I boarded saw me and followed me here. I haven't seen him since then, but he could be lurking around every corner or in every shadow.* Another sound interrupted her thoughts. It was not footsteps that she heard. It was a noise of shuffling feet followed by a thud. She clung to the post, wishing she could dissolve herself inside it. *Wonder what that was? The rule of the ship is all passengers are to clear the promenade deck and be in their staterooms by one o'clock. I am not even supposed to be here, but Malachi and I planned a rendezvous for tonight. When we pull into port at Deauville, France, tomorrow afternoon, we must have well laid out plans.* She jumped as the clock nearby struck two o'clock.

Easing away from the shadow of the post, Deborah carefully edged her way toward the center of the deck. She felt along the sides of a wall until feeling the knob of the door that opened into the ship's library. Not sure of the exact setup and rather than stumble and fall, she lingered just inside the room. As she took a step to clear the doorway, something walloped into her back. Pain mixed with terror raced up and down her spine as the force propelled her farther into the dark room. Completely out of control of her movements, she stumbled forward whamming her side into something solid. Grabbing hold of it to steady herself and realizing it was a desk, she ducked down behind it. Managing to squelch an agonizing scream and before she could catch her breath good, she heard another thud mingled with a groan. Her heart was racing ninety to nothing. She heard a voice.

Unaware that something blocked the doorway to the library, Malachi stumbled and went sprawling flat on his face to the floor. "Ooooh."

That sounds like Malachi. Petrified, Deborah could not force a nerve or sinew to move. Opening her mouth but thinking it best to remain silent for the time being, she clamped it shut and stayed hunched down in her hiding place behind the desk.

Malachi eased himself up. Definitely, that was not the easiest thing he had ever done, considering he had an attaché case handcuffed to his arm. Rubbing his cheek, he felt something wet. *Blood. Oh well.* Wiping the blood on his pants and an expert at moving in the darkness, he maneuvered his way around until reaching a solid object. Running his hand over the smooth surface, he touched a small lantern and switched it on. Sensing another presence in the room, he held the lantern outward and peered behind the desk.

"Deb?" Putting the lantern down, he lifted her up with his free arm and held her close. She was shuddering with fear. "Why are you hiding behind the desk?"

"I…I had just entered the room when something fell and hit my back. It scared me almost senseless. What…what is it?"

"I stumbled over whatever it is and hit the floor. Are you calm enough to check it out?"

"I think so." She picked up the lantern. "You're bleeding, Malachi."

"Just a scratch." Taking her hand, they eased over to the door.

Looking downward, Deborah whispered. "It's a body."

Malachi stooped down. Lifting the victim's wrist, he felt for a pulse. "I'm afraid it is a dead body."

"What are we to do?"

"Number one, we have to get out of here. I told you working with me is too dangerous."

"I am secure, now. All trembling is gone." She squeezed his hand. "I am holding to my anchor."

"Your anchor, as you call me, is not too stable at present. So we both must hold firm to the Anchor that is unshakeable and steadfast. Now, we have to make our way around this dead body. In no way can we get mixed up in a murder." Tiptoeing around the lifeless form that was in a vertical position and blocking the entrance, they came to a sudden halt.

A voice came from outside the library. "Go straight to your staterooms. Now. And not together."

They looked at each other. "Wait here, Deb." Malachi practically ran from the library, pushing aside the fact he was treading on the dead man who was blocking the door. "Sorry, mister," he whispered, "but you are in my way." Stepping onto the deck, he inched slightly away from the door and looked about hoping to spot the person who ordered them back to their rooms. Of course, in the darkness, he could not see if someone was nearby. *The lantern. I left it with Deb. Fine time to think of it now.* He dared a whisper. "Who is it?" When no one replied, he raised his voice. "Is anyone here? If so, please make yourself known."

Somewhat annoyed, he stepped back to the library, but quickly turned around when he heard the sound of hurried footsteps. *I should follow and force an explanation from him, but Deborah comes first.*

THE ANCHOR

"Come on, Deb. We better hurry. Put down the lantern. You can't take it out of the library."

Standing near the dead body, Deborah asked. "Malachi, how am I going to get through the door?"

"Step on him."

"Step on him? A dead man?"

"Yes. He can't hurt you."

"Don't be so heartless."

"Deb, the man is dead. There is no other way. Anyway, we don't know who he is. He may have been dogging us just waiting for the right opportunity to nab us. You go first and do not tarry."

Malachi lingered behind keeping Deborah in his sight until she entered her stateroom and locked the door. Once inside his own room, he took off his belt and slipped his finger into a small opening between the lining and waist band of his pants. He then removed a small key and unlocked the handcuff, giving his arm some reprieve from the attaché case. Although not heavy, it seemed the longer he carried it the heavier it became. After returning the key to its hiding place, he lay across the bed with the case beside him. Wide eyed, he stared up at the ceiling. *I will be glad when this time tomorrow comes, and I can get off this ship. For some reason I feel safer on solid ground. And maybe, just maybe, I can find a way to be with Deb.*

Closing heavy eyelids, he succumbed to drowsiness as his whole body seemed to be overtaken by a stronger force. *He was running on the deck of the mighty Onyx as it was tossing with turbulent waves on the Ouachita River. He was running and hiding between barrels and crates of cargo. The storm was raging and then all was still. He sneaked out from his secret shelter and walked to the edge of the deck. There was a loud boom. Smoke was billowing up from the Onyx. People were screaming and running. Sabotaged! The ship has been sabotaged! He put his right hand over his heart feeling the leather pouch, knowing he was responsible for keeping it safe at all cost. He knew there was only one thing to do. He jumped into the dashing waters as one more loud boom sounded, and parts of the mighty Onyx split into smithereens as it sank to a watery grave.*

Chapter 24

Awakened out of a deep sleep, Malachi opened his eyes, but quickly closed them again when a feeling of zigzagging from one place to another overpowered him. Daring a look through squinched eyes, he uttered, "What in the world is wrong with me? I was dreaming about the sinking of the Onyx. It was rocking and reeling, and then it exploded." The realization that it was the SS Atlantic, and not the Onyx, that was on turbulent waters, jarred him back fully to the present. As the bed shifted one way and then another, he grabbed the headboard with a tenacious hold while his body swerved back and forth on the veering bed. His efforts were in vain as the twisting and turning caused him to lose grip, sending him to the floor and reeling across the room. Slamming into the wall, he lay there with face to the floor, temporarily rendered senseless. At last, discerning the fact that he was not caught up in some kind of whimsical vision, but what he was feeling was reality, he pushed against the floor with both hands. It seemed that every muscle and joint was out of whack and would not cooperate. Closing his eyes, he dropped his head against folded arms and fought back the dizziness that tried to possess him.

Feeling as if he had just gotten off a merry-go-round, with as much energy as he could muster up, once again he pushed against the floor with both hands and managed to get to his knees. Knowing to try and stand on his feet was useless, he crawled across the floor to the bed. Grabbing the footboard, he clung to it trying to steady himself, which was hopeless since the ship was still tossing and turning. Holding on for dear life, he uttered, "I have to check on Deb. I must go to her room." With hands still on the bed, he eased his way to the side nearest the door but was arrested as the Captain's voice came booming through the speaking trumpet, overpowering the noise of the ship.

"Attention all passengers." The Captain spoke with authority and Malachi detected a sense of urgency in his voice. "I am sure some of you are upset, and some maybe are afraid. I want to assure you, all is under control. We ran into a storm, as you probably already know. The ship is not damaged. No harm done unless perhaps a few broken dishes in the kitchen, and other items which I believe have changed locations. But that is minor. No lives lost. Stay in your stateroom to ensure your own safety. Some of my staff will be checking on each of you. So don't wander around on deck or elsewhere."

A loud knock sounded and the door opened before Malachi could answer. A man dressed in the ship's uniform stepped inside. Holding a lantern up and out, he glanced around the room. "You okay in here? Well, it is obvious the room is a bit disheveled." Focusing the light on Malachi, he continued, "And from all appearances, so are you." His gazed rested on the attaché case, which through all the swerving and twisting had been hurled to the floor and was resting against the bureau.

Malachi followed his gaze, thankful that he was closer to the case should the man decide to do more than simply look. "I'm all right. It is not me I am worried about."

The man stood in the doorway averting his eyes from Malachi. "Who are you worried about?"

Malachi squelched the dare to voice his thoughts. *I wish you would leave and go about your business so I can see for myself.* He asked, "Uh...uh are all the other passengers okay?"

Staring at him, the man asked, "Why are you so interested?"

"Because I care about other people."

"Really," the man said. He stepped into the hall and walked away, leaving Malachi standing dumbfounded in the complete darkness.

Malachi eased along the side of the bed to the headboard. Realizing the lantern was probably shattered into bits and pieces, he made his way to the small bureau and picked up the attaché case. Opening the shallow drawer of the bureau and fumbling around inside, he took out some matches. Striking one, it offered little light but would have to do. "Ouch," he gasped as a burning seared his finger. Throwing down what was left of the short stem of the match, he shook his hand and touched his finger to his tongue to cool it down some. After attaching the case to his arm, he moved as fast as he could to the door and stepped from his room into the hall.

Not seeing any sign of the man who had just left him in the dark, he hugged the wall supporting himself with one hand. Although the sailing was still somewhat rough, the ship seemed a little steadier. Making his way down the hall, just as he rounded the corner to the other staterooms, he saw the man step from Deborah's room and close the door. Quickly, he ducked back around the corner and waited. Sneaking a brief look and not seeing the man, he hurried down the hall and knocked on Deborah's door. She did not respond. Trying the knob, fortunately, it turned and he entered the room anxious to get out of sight.

The dim light of a small lantern cast a glow inside the room. All was quiet. "Deb? Deb, are you here? It's Malachi."

Deborah stepped from a small closet and flung herself into him. In a state of panic, she clung to him, fiercely.

Putting his free arm around her, he whispered, "Now, now. You are all right. Everything is fine. The ship has settled down."

"What a dreadful experience. My first time to sail and to be caught up in the middle of a disastrous storm is so horrifying. It was so dark. Someone put a lantern on the bureau, fumbled around and restored some order to the room."

"I had to be sure you are okay. I am really not supposed to be here you know. So with great remorse, and reluctantly, I had better get back to my own room." He squeezed her tightly then walked to the door. Stepping into the hall, at the sound of the Captain's voice, quickly he stepped back into Deborah's room.

"I want to clarify further and put your minds at ease. Because of the heavy south and westerly gales that beset us, we had to slow the ship down to conserve fuel. This will delay our arrival at France by one day, hopefully no longer."

Malachi clutched the attaché case against his body. He looked at Deborah. "When I finally get rid of this thing, I will feel free as bird out of its cage."

"What is in it?" Deborah questioned.

"Well.." He stopped talking as the Captain continued.

"Also, I commend the pilots for guiding the ship slowly but safely through the gale force winds, over turbulent waters and intermittent visibility. At times they had to heave to and fix the helm and sailing positions so the vessel did not have to be steered. This, also, caused a delay in progress until the strongest and contrary winds had past. We are moving, again. Darkness has overtaken us. Since we will be sailing during the night hours, no one should be ambling about on deck. It will be to your advantage to obey orders and remain in your own room until we dock at France."

"You better go, Malachi."

Satisfied that Deborah was all right and the ship seemed to be moving rather smoothly, Malachi stepped into the hall and hurried to his quarters. Entering the dark room, he felt an avalanche of overwhelming danger. Striking a match, he looked about and stood as if frozen in place. Sheets were stripped from the bed and lay in a heap against one wall. The mattress now had a big gash down the middle and hung over the footboard. His undergarments and other personal things decorated the room from one side to the other. "Wow!" He touched the attaché case. "It's you they want." A wham on the head caused him to stumble. "But they won't get…" He sank to the floor no longer conscious of the darkness that encircled him.

He heard voices. They were very distant and muffled. As consciousness slowly eased its way back, his body became aware of its present situation. He was on top of the attaché case which felt like it was partly imbedded into his left side, while the hard floor, supporting the rest of his weight, seemed to be poking into every fiber of his being. Realizing the voices he heard were in his room, he resisted the urge to move his aching body. Although still somewhat incoherent but straining to understand what was being said, he felt a presence hovering over him. Someone picked up his free arm.

"Is he dead?" The voice was clear and distinct.

"No. His pulse rate is okay," was the reply. "It is a good thing he isn't or I would be when the Captain found out."

"What are you going to do with him?"

"Well…" The man paused. "At the last meeting, the Captain said we may have to throw him overboard, if it becomes necessary for his safety."

"What? You must be kidding."

"The Captain doesn't kid about government security. Of course, that would be the last resort."

Throw me overboard? Malachi released a groan and lifted his head. "Stop talking about me as if I'm not here. Over my dead body will you throw me overboard."

The man helped Malachi to a sitting position. "If we don't do something, that is exactly what we are going to have. Your dead body. We have already had one murder and for sure don't want another one."

"I know. I stumbled over the dead man," Malachi replied. "Who was he?"

"Who he was is not important, now, but to keep you safe is. A word of caution, it could have just as easily been you."

"Who killed him then?"

The man ignored the question. "Can you walk? The Captain wants to see you."

Chapter 25

Staring out across the ocean, Deborah leaned against the deck railing. The reflection of the sun's rays against the ripples of the water caused a glistening effect like sparkling stars resting upon a layer of drifting ice. Her ears perked up at the sound of the Captain's voice.

"We have just entered the English Channel and will be docking at the Port of Deauville, France, in two hours. From here on, it should be smooth sailing. However, as we advance in the Channel there will be intermit heavy fog at times, greatly affecting visibility. It is to our advantage we are crossing during daylight hours but still may have to slow our speed for safety purposes."

Deborah turned her attention back to the watery path before her. Thinking about the horrible storm they had just gone through made her appreciate the present tranquility even more. After what she had experienced over the past months, the words of the motto at home were forever embedded in her heart and mind. Spontaneously, she uttered, "The Anchor holds in spite of the storm." She thought of the small anchor she had found in Dorsey's Store. *It really was of no importance. Just a small piece of iron someone didn't want. But I wanted it. So did Malachi. To us it symbolizes Jesus, the Rock, the Anchor. The only reliable and sure One we can cling to with the uncertainty that confronts us seemingly every minute and everywhere we go.*

Although thankful for the peace after the storm, her mind refused to succumb to the stillness. *Wonder where Malachi is? I thought he would be on deck by now. Maybe when we finally arrive in France, we can see more of each other.* As anxiety encroached its way into her mind, she clutched the railing with both hands and stood erect. "Where is he?" Her voice was filled with emotion. She fought for self-control, struggling to keep hysteria from overpowering her. With searching eyes, she craned her neck to see above and around some of the other passengers who were mingling on deck. Dealing with a mixture of mental distress and fear that Malachi had not shown himself as they had planned, agitation refused to flee. Deciding movement may help, she walked slowly along the railing stopping at intervals hoping to get a glimpse of him. Reluctantly, she maneuvered her way toward the middle of the deck weaving in and out among the throne of people who were thoroughly enjoying the freedom of no longer being confined to small staterooms. As if the absence of Malachi was not enough to deal with at the moment, an unwelcome image of the man who had confronted her earlier on the voyage forced its way in and niggled away at her brain. *What if that man happens up again and tries to force me to go with him?* With that thought and wanting to avoid another unpleasant encounter, she decided it best to return to her room.

Deborah paced back and forth, hoping Malachi would somehow make it to her room without being seen. At the sound of any voice or footsteps outside her door, she rushed and opened it slightly, only to be disappointed. No longer able to endure the boredom and suspense, she decided to go back on deck. After glancing both ways of the hall, and not wanting to mingle with other passengers, quietly and inconspicuously, she headed toward Malachi's room. Just as she reached his door, to her dismay a man approached her. Quickly pretending to be searching for something in her reticule, she kept her head lowered. To her relief he tipped his hat with a quick, "How do you do, Mam," and continued down the hall.

"Whew," she breathed. "I am thankful he didn't want to be too friendly." Being sure the coast was clear, she lifted her hand to knock on the door but noticed it was slightly ajar. Hesitating momentarily, she opened it a little wider and whispered, "Malachi?" There was no reply. She listened. Not hearing a sound, she stepped inside the room, closed the door gently and stood transfixed. Her mouth flew open in horror, but no words came. Her head was swimming. Her body was swaying. Somehow, she managed to utter, "The ship is reeling and tossing. We must have sailed into another storm." Leaning against the door, she slowly sank to the floor. Taking deep breaths, she stayed there until feeling somewhat normal. Reality hit. It was not the ship but a sudden violent and mental disturbance had attacked her, leaving her equilibrium temporarily unbalanced. Slowly she got back on her feet and looked around. "What a disheveled mess. Someone broke in here and searched this room. The only way they could get what they want was to take Malachi." As those words sank in on her, she released a whimpered wail. "Oh no!"

Hearing footsteps, Deborah stepped quickly to the side so if someone entered she would be hidden behind the door. Flattening herself against the wall, she waited, hardly daring to breathe. The footsteps ceased. Someone was at the door. Already as close to the wall as possible, she held her breath, knowing it was not Malachi for he would walk in. The door opened. Although unable to see, she knew someone had entered the room. She waited. *Wish I could make myself invisible right now.* She inflated her jaws trying to hold her breath longer. Feeling she may explode at any moment and become a mere heap on the floor, she gradually exhaled. Seeing the door slowly closing, she breathed a sigh of relief. To her chagrin, the door opened again, wider than before. It swung back using her body for a door stop and sending her reticule to the floor. She clenched her teeth to keep from releasing a screaming yell, knowing she could do nothing but wait. She heard a loud, "Hmm."

That is a man's voice. Wonder what he is doing? He must be pilfering through Malachi's things. Then recognizing a sound, she knew the intruder had put the mattress back in its rightful place and none too gently from the lingering vibration of the bedsprings. Once more there was silence. *Who is he? It is too quiet. I wonder what he wants.* She didn't have to wonder long, for to her dismay, the door moved, slowly at first then flung away from her so quickly all she could do was stand frozen in place as two piercing eyes bored into her. Deborah didn't move but returned the look, stare to stare.

The man's voice was stern. "What are you doing in here?"

An unseen hand seemed to touch her, giving her confidence and stability. Feeling completely in control, Deborah refused to be intimidated by the man's voice or his stare. She proceeded to brush off her clothes, straighten her hair, and since he made no effort to do so, picked up her reticule. *I could ask you the same thing.* However, keeping her thoughts to herself, she walked with head high and shoulders erect to the center of the room.

"Wait a minute," the man said hastily. "I want to know what you are doing in this room."

I know I have seen this man a few times while sailing, but he is not the one that tried to force his company on me. I don't want to lie. What can I say without revealing important information. Deborah looked at him. "The young man who stays in this room has kept me company a few times on this voyage. I got bored and thought I would seek him out. When he didn't respond to my knock, the door was slightly ajar, so I came in." Endeavoring to turn attention from herself, she asked, "Are you responsible for this mess?"

"I have no intention of answering any of your nosey questions. I am telling you to get out of this room right now, before I pick you up and throw you out."

Deborah gave him a defiant look. "You wouldn't dare."

"Oh wouldn't I?" The man moved quickly to her side and picked her up.

"Put me down. Put me down."

"Be quiet. I am about to." He deposited her just outside the room. "If you value your life, mind your own business." He closed the door behind them. "And stay away from the man that occupies this room." Without another word, he walked away.

Deborah stared at his back. Having somewhat of a defiant spirit, she was very tempted to go back inside the room. Knowing Malachi's mission was of utmost importance and not wanting to bring him harm, she decided against it and walked toward her own stateroom. *Maybe I should report this to the Captain. No, I can't do that. We are not supposed to even know each other. Get hold of yourself, Deborah Dotson. Oh where is he? That man knew something but wouldn't tell me.* Too disturbed to return to her room, she turned and made her way back around the staterooms heading to her usual spot beside the safety railing, hoping Malachi would be there. He was not. She paced back and forth. Her heart was pounding. Her thoughts were pressing. *It is imperative that I find Malachi. He is somewhere on this ship. But where?*

Chapter 26

Miserable and in a quandary as to what to do next and where to look for Malachi, Deborah continued pacing the deck floor fighting for self-control. She paused, leaned against a support column and willed herself to dismiss every negative and scary thought that threatened her sanity. With eyes closed she did not move even a muscle. In that moment of stillness, an idea popped into her mind. Making her way to the stairs, she quickly descended to the lower deck and looked about. No one was stirring. *Good, I don't have to be concerned about being calm and inconspicuous.* With that thought, hurrying around stacks of freight and other necessary ship supplies, she went straight to the safety rail.

Thinking that maybe she had misunderstood since they had met secretly on the lower deck once before, Deborah walked along the railing. She paused near a small platform that extended beyond the deck resisting the temptation to step onto it. *That may not be a sensible thing to do considering the only protection from falling straight into the ocean is a short cable.* So absorbed in her thoughts, she was unaware that someone had crept up behind her. Rough hands forced her down and, before she could release a scream, pushed her over the edge of the platform feet first. She grabbed hold of the cable with both hands. She yelled, "Help! Help me! Help…" Her cry for help was cut short when a foot pushed her head under the water. Managing to pull herself up enough so her face was above surface, she screamed, "Somebody help me." The foot was on her head again pushing her under. It stopped. Kicking against the current, she managed to surface again. She heard a commotion above her. Then strong arms grabbed her pulling her back onto the platform.

THE ANCHOR

Shivering, she leaned against her rescuer. In a broken and weak voice, she whispered, "Oh. Oh, someone tried to kill me."

Holding her in a warm embrace, a voice whispered, "Now, now, it's over. You are all right. You are safe."

There was no mistaking that voice. "Now I am. Oh, Malachi, will we ever be out of harm's way?"

He could not resist the urge to hold her close for a brief moment. "You had better get back upstairs to your room and get into dry clothes before someone sees you. Can you make it by yourself?"

"I can. I am all right now."

He helped her to her feet. "Okay, but hurry. Please stay in your room, Deb."

Deborah turned and walked toward the steps leading to the middle deck. Venturing one more look back, Malachi was standing on the platform at the place where she had been pushed into the ocean. He appeared to be examining the safety cable. She saw a man walk up beside him. The man was saying something. Deborah strained to hear what he was saying but could not distinguish a word. Not believing her eyes, she stared in horror and rushed forward just as the man picked Malachi up. She screamed. "Malachi!"

⚓⚓⚓

With one hand on his belt and the other the seat of his pants, a man whispered, "Are you ready for this, Malachi Hebron?"

"Let me think…"

"No time to think." The man launched him into outer space like an arrow toward its target. The last words of his assailant bellowed over the sound of the ocean waves. "Sink or swim!"

Malachi heard another voice. A desperate scream. *That's Deb. She wasn't supposed to see this. Deb, I am sorry. I was not allowed to warn you.*

Suddenly, like a sack of rocks, he hit the surface of the deepest blue he had ever seen. The waters parted leaving him surrounded by a ring of swirling ripples. Lifting his head above water, he gave it a good hard shake and grabbed hold of the attaché case with his free hand. "Glad you are not heavy. If you were, the great Atlantic Ocean would swallow us up as if we were a lead sinker on a fishing line." He watched as the big sailing vessel that had been his home for weeks moved forward without him. He was sure there were two forms staring at him from the lower deck. The man who threw him overboard and Deborah. He whispered, "Don't worry, Deb. I will see you soon."

The sound of her voice calling his name echoed across the waves. "Malachi! Malachi! Mala..!" Deborah kept screaming until a hand clamped over her mouth and a strong arm flung around her waist. She continued to call his name although it was only a muffled sound. With both hands she clawed at the one covering her mouth, but it didn't budge. In a state of panic and hysteria, despair overpowered her. The SS Atlantic moved forward toward its destination until the swirling ripples and the man she loved were completely out of sight. She stopped struggling, submitting to helplessness.

The man released her and removed his hand from her mouth. "If you know what is good for you, you will be mum about this little incident that you were privy to. Of all the nosey people." The man's voice faded into nothingness as Deborah went limp and collapsed on the deck floor in a dead faint.

Deborah opened her eyes. Everything appeared hazy, as if she were in a daze. *What happened to me? I don't remember. I am on the bed. I don't remember lying down.* She closed her eyes tightly. Suddenly things became clearer as her thought pattern aligned with reality. She opened her eyes and sat upright on the bed. "Malachi," she whispered. "A man threw him into the Atlantic Ocean. Whoever he was warned me to keep quiet. I fainted and someone brought me to my room." Determined, she got up from the bed. "That is strange that I was warned to stay mum about a man being thrown overboard. What kind of person do they think I am, anyway. I am going straight to the Captain."

Feeling like a disheveled mess, she walked over to take a look at herself in a small mirror hanging above the bureau. A folded piece of paper on top of the bureau caught her eye. She picked it up, unfolded it and stood transfixed while reading the message it contained. "Oh," she breathed clutching the note to her chest. Weak in her knees, she sat down on the bed and read the note again, aloud and slowly, letting it sink in on her. "Don't worry about Malachi. The incident you witnessed was planned. It was necessary for his own safety. You will reunite on land. Instructions are waiting for you at Port Deauville." She bowed her head and with the opened note across her palms buried her face in her hands. Mixed emotions swept over her. Although thankful that Malachi would be rescued and very soon they would be together, the image of him being thrown overboard into the Atlantic Ocean flashed before her bringing fear and uncertainty of what lay ahead for them. Alone in her room, she no longer had to pretend that all was well and mask bravery. With both hands in her lap and clutching the note as tears rolled down her cheeks, Deborah prayed until all the frustration and fear she had experienced the past hour were replaced with calmness and a peace she could not explain.

The SS Atlantic moved onward toward the coast of France leaving Malachi farther and farther behind to deal with the situation as best he could. *What do they expect me to do. Just bobble around in this water. No way. This is the second time I have been plunged to a watery grave. Well, the first time was my choice, but this time someone decided for me.*

Although the attaché case was light, it was somewhat of a hindrance. Thinking fast and moving swiftly, he started swimming in the same direction as the ship. The technique of swimming with one arm had been part of his training. Confident, yet anxious, he swam with one arm strokes, his left arm and the case stretched out before him. One arm swimming made it more pertinent that he concentrate and think clearly with decisive relevance and not let his mind wander. He could not prevent the memories that clouded his thinking. He remembered that cold day in February when he jumped overboard in the raging, icy waters of the Ouachita River and the sinking of the mighty Onyx before his very eyes. Engulfed in a watery mass, he thought of his nice warm bed at Bethel and the constant care of Momma and Zip. Vexing, indeed, was the fact it was not the Ouachita that was about to swallow him up but the English Channel, a part of the enormous Atlantic Ocean that connected two continents.

Swimming slowly in the path as the ocean liner, which now was only a speck on the horizon, Malachi wondered about the life boat that should have already come to his rescue. Both arms were tiring. One from swimming and the other from being stretched out before him with the attaché case cuffed to it. *This is not the easiest thing I have ever done.* He stopped swimming, satisfied just to bobbed up and down since it required less energy. Scheduled to arrive in France by the end of the day on the SS Atlantic was history for him.

Chapter 27

Although anxious to leave the ocean liner, the incidents earlier in the day had perturbed Deborah emotionally and drained her temporarily of will and energy to push herself into action. She had not the vim or vitality to force her body to move, nor the ability to squelch her overactive mind. *What I thought was to be an exciting and enjoyable adventure to France, turned into a nightmare. It was exciting all right, but not the way I hoped. Somebody tried to drown me, and Malachi was thrown overboard. I still think they could have come up with a better way to protect him, from whomever or whatever.* Just thinking about it made her shutter.

By the time she finally pulled herself together enough to collect all of her things and leave her room, the disembarking area was already crowded with excited passengers ready to exit their moving home. Standing on the deck of the SS Atlantic waiting to go ashore, she stretched herself on tiptoes, craning her neck trying to see above heads of those in front of her. Quite a way down the line and a bit disgusted with herself for being so slothful, she looked upward. Her eyes rested on a mast that towered high in the air with a Stars and Stripes flag blowing in the breeze. She smiled in spite of the harrying escapades in which her and Malachi's lives had been threatened. Realizing she was about to step onto foreign soil and would no longer be on homeland security and protected under the America flag, the smile vanished as a feeling of dread swept over her. Unaware that she had not moved forward in line leaving quite a distance between her and the passenger in front, she was startled by a male voice behind her.

"Miss, are you all right? If not, we will get the medic. Otherwise, will you please move forward before I step in front of you."

"Sorry." Deborah quickly moved forward. In a much lower tone, she uttered, "Guess I had better concentrate on the present otherwise I may receive another reprimand." Nevertheless, there came a response from behind her.

"Now what is your problem?"

Deborah turned, forced a smile and looked at the passenger. "Feel free to step in front of me, sir. However, I seriously doubt it would be of much benefit."

The man harrumphed and motioned for her to move forward.

Arriving at the gangplank and putting one hand on the side rail, Deborah dismissed all thoughts of the disgruntled man behind her. Putting a hand across her chest, she cast a glance toward the bow of the ship wanting one more look at the beautiful Stars and Stripes towering above the highest peak of the ocean liner. However, it was not the flag that caused her to gasp but the man leaning against the support pole staring at her. Clutching at her heart, she felt incapable of moving. Her legs felt heavy as if lead weights were chained to them. *It's him. It is the man who tried to force his company on me. Thought I was rid of him.*

So distraught with her eyes fixed on the man, she was unaware that other passengers were sidestepping her and hurrying down the gangplank. Abruptly, the man walked away from the pole and headed toward her. Still feeling a bit befuddled, the weights that had rendered her unmovable earlier disappeared as she moved into action. Without another backward glance, she hurried down the gangplank, her brain bombarded with questions that had no answers. A perplexity of unsettling thoughts wrapped around her mind. *I can't panic. At the moment, my one desire is to get as far away from that pest as possible and do it now.*

Deborah moved quickly away from the gangplank trying to lose herself in the crowd. Needing to come to grips with her emotions, she stopped walking, closed her eyes, took a deep breath and then released it slowly, relishing the fact at long last she was off the SS Atlantic. "It is so good to be standing on solid ground, again," she uttered. "Good old terra firma." She jumped when a hand touched her shoulder. Afraid to open her eyes for fear she had tarried too long and the man from the ship had her in his clutches at last, she quenched her eyelids tighter together.

She didn't budge until a voice whispered, "You are safe."

Keeping one eye closed, she peeked at the man beside her. Opening the other eye, she blinked and barely afforded a smile of relief that it was not the man who had made her so uncomfortable, although she had no clue who was standing beside her. Stealing a glance backward, with searching eyes she looked for the man who appeared to be dogging her every move, yet seemed to become invisible at will. There was no sign of him.

The man who had stepped up beside her spoke. "You are in France, now. No time for loitering."

"But…but, that person back there. He was on the ship the whole time. Is he the one who tried to drown me? Why did he want to kill me? Who is he?"

"That is not important," the man replied. "Is this your bag?"

Ignoring his question, Deborah gave him an incredible look. "But that man tried to kill me!"

"Forget it. As I have already said, you are safe, and it is my duty to keep you so and get you to the place of rendezvous." With her bag in tow the man started walking away from the port.

Skepticism held her steadfast. She didn't move. "Are you French? You speak perfect English."

The man stopped, but ignored her question. "We are going into the city of Deauville. It is part of the Calvados of Normandy. Only a brief walk. Come along."

With guarded precaution, Deborah stepped up beside him. "I suppose I should be more concerned at the present with who you are and where you are taking me. How do I know you can be trusted?"

"You have to trust me. At the moment, you have no other choice."

"Where is Malachi? I thought he was to meet me here."

The man gave her a blank stare. "Malachi? Who is Malachi? I have no idea where he is. Whoever he is."

"Aren't you supposed to give me a passcode?"

"Passcode? I know nothing about a passcode."

Deborah stared into the man's blank expression. She may as well have been staring at a stone wall. *Does he really not know anything? If he does, he has certainly mastered the art of ignorance.*

For a brief moment the man held her gaze. Then shrugging his shoulders, he started walking letting her know he had nothing more to say.

Deborah took a couple of skips to catch up with him then walked in silence while many still unanswered questions racked her brain. *I want some answers. I need some answers.* Casting an inconspicuous glance at her escort, she pondered. *The problem is, I don't know how much he knows. How do I approach him. Suppose he doesn't know Malachi. Suppose he doesn't know anything about why I am in France. Suppose he is simply obeying an order to get me safely to someone who does know. Or… suppose… he is leading me straight into a trap.* The words of her training instructor flashed through her mind like a large red warning sign. *Trust no one. Trust no one.*

For her safety and her escort's, if he was completely unaware of any misdoings, Deborah thought it best to honor his dismissal sign and steer the conversation away from her and the reason she was in France. Wanting to clear her thoughts, she decided to break the silence. "You said Deauville is part of the Calvados of Normandy? What is the Calvados?"

The man actually smiled. Who would ever have thought the same man a few minutes earlier had just given her a blank stare as if she were nothing more than a nosey busybody. "Calvados is actually a drink made from apple cider but not just any apple cider. The cider must come from specially grown and selected apples known as the Calvados apples. The Calvados cider is a very supreme drink in all of France, especially along the coast and Paris. I will caution you. If you want to try it, be sure to drink the freshly brewed which is just a refreshing drink. Once aged, it is a type of brandy and will render you very intoxicated."

Deborah was now the one with a blank stare. So befuddled and preoccupied with thoughts of who this strange man could be and where he was taking her, she paid no attention to her surroundings until they turned onto a narrow path. It appeared to be well used, but the farther they walked, the more apprehensive she became. It seemed she was being led deeper and deeper into isolation. They finally came to a small quaint building, which did nothing to ease her qualms.

"Well, here we are. This is where I leave you," her escort explained.

"Leave me? What is this place?"

"It is a cider house, or some had rather call it a distillery." He put the bag on the ground, opened the door and motioned for her to precede him inside. Lingering in the doorway, he said, "Wait here until you receive further instructions." Without another word, he stepped out of the building.

Deborah watched him walk away. *I still don't know if he was friend or enemy.* She stood near the door of the rustic building so, if necessary, she could make a quick exit. The dampness and dim lighting were very forbidding. The odor was ghastly, unlike anything she had ever smelled before. Covering her mouth and nose with her hand, she released a muffled, "Ugh." The stillness and silence only added to her dread. Feeling lost in the middle of nowhere, it seemed as if a dozen hammers were pounding inside her. Standing transfixed until hearing a voice which made her jump, she whirled around and came face to face with a young man.

Evidently, he thought an introduction was unnecessary. "I am to escort you to the depot where you will board the train to Paris." He stepped outside the building and picked up her bag. "Come with me. We must hurry."

Deborah had no choice and she was glad to be out of the smelly place. "Aren't you supposed to give me the passcode?"

Hurrying along, the young man had kept his eyes straight ahead, but at those words he gave her a side look. "I know nothing about a passcode. Trust me."

Deborah's mind was doing somersaults. *Here is someone else I don't know. He doesn't know the passcode but wants me to trust him. So much for the words of warning. Trust no one. Trust no one. What a pickle I am in. No one told me how to deal with a situation like this.*

Following the young man back along the same path that had led her to the cider house, Deborah was surprised when he turned onto a path less worn. Her escort walked ahead of her pushing aside bushes and tramping down tall weeds. The fact that he was trying to make walking easier for her did nothing to erase the question marks dancing around in her brain. Reaching a clearing, she saw Deauville in the distance. They walked along the outskirts of a city which was only sand dunes until a wealthy man had a vision that he made a reality. A place that once was nothing but wasteland became a city of very expensive real estate due to someone who was bold enough to make a dream come true. Now, it attracted tourists from all over the world. Large villas adorned the once desolate coastal city. Because of the unique architect some resembled ancient castles although built very modern. Allurement and trade were so abundant a railroad was built to carry passengers directly from Deauville into Paris.

Arriving at the depot, Deborah accepted another folded piece of paper. "Your instructions, Mam. Once you are settled on the train, read it carefully and put it in a protective place, then destroy it when you arrive in Paris."

Chapter 28

The life boat that finally rescued Malachi from the English Channel was really nothing more than a fishing vessel. However, the how and means he was bailed out of a very perilous situation was trivial at the moment. There were more important things awaiting him. Standing on the coastline of Brest, France, he watched the dinghy which had saved him from drowning slowly drift away from shore. The sculler of the small vessel lifted a hand in farewell then picked up two long oars and slowly moved the boat out into deeper water. Malachi could tell he was master of the task as the seaman picked up speed, seemingly with little effort.

Standing a short distance from the water, he took note of his appearance. "I am still soaking wet, although not dripping. Thank God for small blessings." He bent down and opened his bag, which by some means had been carried from the ocean liner to the rescue boat and was now resting on the sand at his feet. Taking out the pistol that was carefully hidden between his clothes, he crammed it into the pocket of his wet shirt and looked longingly at his dry clothes. Knowing he had to change before meeting with his contact, he looked about. There was nothing insight that offered any privacy.

Carrying the attaché case in one hand and his bag in the other, he leaned forward struggling to walk in the wet, soggy sand and maneuvered his way from the coastline. When his feet touched solid ground, Malachi took a deep breath of relief and quickened his pace. Arriving at the central point of the small coastal town, a sign grabbed his attention.

"Gig for hire. Hmm. Okay, but from where I stand, it doesn't look like it will go very fast or very far." Approaching the strange looking contraption, he saw a weird shaped vehicle with two small seats on top of two wheels and only one horse to move it. Giving it a closer look, he quickly realized his first impression was probably right. "Looks more like a smaller version of the sulky two row planter Papa bought to plow the fields at Bethel." He released a chuckle. "I am certain the sulky would be faster."

At the sound of a strange voice, he looked down into the face of a small swiveled up human. Although Malachi's French was limited, it was quite obvious the man wanted a customer.

"Do.. you.. understand.. English?" Malachi asked with emphasis on every word.

"Oui. Comme ci, comme ca." With his sparse understanding of French, Malachi knew the man meant yes, so-so.

"How.. much.. to.. Quimper?"

The little man walked around Malachi observing his damp, disheveled clothes. His eyes bulged even wider when he saw the attaché case. "Ten francs, Monsieur."

Malachi handed the man two dollars and climbed onto the gig. The driver hopped up beside him and uttering something in French gave the horse a hard flap with the reins. The animal took off before Malachi could get his bearings good, slinging him forward then backward and giving him an unwelcome whiplash. Without a doubt, he was in for a precarious ride.

After hours of jostling and weaving back and forth, wondering if he was going to reach his destination all in one piece or even get there at all, the gig finally came to a stop. Practically having held his breath the whole miserable trip, Malachi exhaled deeply, stepped to the ground and wiped his brow. He waved goodbye to his rather amusing chauffeur who had refused to take him into the town. Walking in a southerly direction, he entered Quimper, the capital of the most westerly coastline of France. Immediately arrested by two spires towering 250 feet in the air, he was struck by the splendor of a cross resting at the acme of each. "Wow. The famous Cathedral of Saint-Corentin. Only about half the height of the Washington Monument, it is still very impressive."

Walking along the main thoroughfare, he beheld a town with a rustic atmosphere yet very sophisticated. He walked across a footbridge which was only one of several that spanned rivers flowing through the town. There were houses built of half timber and half stone. There were crepey looking shops of various sizes and shapes. In the distance he beheld ruins of historic town walls that had withstood the devastation of centuries. An idea popped into his head. *Among the ruins may be the best place to change without having to reply to nosey questions, suspicious looks and raised eyebrows.* Hastening to the nearest one, Malachi stepped into a small niche in a protruding wall and quickly rid himself of his disheveled clothes. Feeling a bit more self-confident and better about his appearance, he retraced his steps to the main hub of the town.

Arriving at the Cathedral, he was awe-struck by the Gothic-style and the ancient stained glass windows that embellished the building. Although he would have liked to tour inside the magnificent edifice, he didn't tarry but walked across the square to a building located opposite the Cathedral. His place of contact, the Museum of Arts, somewhat different in appearance from the Saint-Corentin, was just as interesting. Designed with a nineteenth century facade, the building had its own attractive identity, portraying the style of an Italian urban palace.

Malachi entered the building through an arched doorway. Several large rooms graced the first floor. The captain had given him instructions shortly before he was dumped overboard. *Go straight to the art gallery and wait.* There was no sign pointing to or identifying the gallery, but it was easily spotted. He stepped into a room lit with skylights and was amazed at the various splendid paintings.

THE ANCHOR

Aimlessly, he moved among the displayed art collection with anticipation that soon he would be on his way to Paris. Smoothing his hand over the lock of the attaché case and the cuff that was linked to his arm, he stopped in front of a painting by the famous artist, Silguy. Becoming more anxious and irritable by each fleeting moment, he waited. From all appearances, he was the only one in the gallery. No proprietor seemed to be manning the place.

Wondering if maybe he had been given the wrong instructions and debating whether to wait a while longer, he noticed a movement in his peripheral vision. Turning his attention in that direction, he watched as a man approached. The man handed him an envelope and without uttering a word, turned and walked away. Malachi glared at the man's back. He had already learned from past experiences, if his contact had nothing to say there was no need for questions. Opening the envelope, he took out a folded piece of paper. Tucked inside was a note with directions scribbled across the front, a train ticket to Paris, and brief but explicit information for when he arrived. Noticing the departure time on the ticket, he looked at the note with directions to the depot. In bold letters were the words HURRY! TRAIN DEPARTS SHORTLY!

Hastening from the gallery, Malachi muttered, "They make me wait for the longest, and then I have to rush like a track runner to arrive at the station before the train rumbles away without me." Once outside the museum, he did run, with bag in one hand and the handle of the attaché case in the other. Having to slow his pace among the hustle and bustle of the business hub of the town, he weaved in and out among mothers pushing baby carriages, while others were just out for leisurely walks. Some were moving at a snail pace and loafers dawdled along without purpose or direction.

Hastening over one footbridge and then another, at last he caught a glimpse of the depot. He stopped running, bent over and took a deep breath. The whistle of the train brought him quickly upright and moving again. The train was leaving. *I'll never make it. This is the last train to Paris today. If someone had not been dragging their feet I wouldn't be in this predicament.* To his surprise the train stopped. He kept his eyes glued in that direction. The conductor stepped off the train onto the platform, shaded his eyes, then turned and appeared to be speaking to someone hidden from Malachi's view. Momentarily, the conductor stepped back onto the train. When Malachi reached the platform, the whistle sounded again. He could not resist a glance around and just in time to see a man step into view. *It is the man who handed me the envelope.*

The man tipped his hat then turned and walked away. Malachi stared once again at the back of the person who had shown him no interest, yet felt it necessary to delay the train until he made it to the depot. The blasting of the whistle brought him to attention, and the train moved out just as Malachi hopped aboard.

After taking his ticket, the conductor gave Malachi a questioning look then focused on the case handcuffed to his arm. "You almost missed this train. You look too young to be somebody important, but I reckon you are. Your friend held this train up until you got here. Thanks to him, you will get to Paris today."

Malachi took the nearest available seat. *My friend? Just like so many others I have encountered since leaving America, I haven't the faintest clue who he is.*

Chapter 29

Standing on the platform of the Nord Train Rail Lines in Paris, France, Malachi beheld in amazement the place once known to all as the city of lights. Having never been to Paris, he tried to imagine what it must have been like before it was greatly transformed due to a five month siege by the Germans. Kowing Paris was the most coveted and prestigious location in France, he could hardly comprehend that this once beautiful city had served as the camping grounds for French soldiers, National Guardsmen, and volunteers who refused German rule. They had chosen to defend their city although it was heavily besieged by Prussian forces. The Franco-Prussian War, which crippled France during 1870-1871, had left its mark. Although the prolonged siege had debilitated the city economically, it did not alter the spirit of the people. Walking along the same streets that German soldiers had tromped upon a year prior to his coming, he was very aware of the busy French people working diligently to restore their city of lights to its former beauty.

Malachi knew all too well the devastating aftermath of a war torn country. Looking around, he whispered, "It is inconceivable that enemy troops marched right down the main thoroughfare of this city, after bombarding it when the French refused to be coerced into surrender by starvation."

Making his way along the main thoroughfare of the city, Malachi stopped at intervals and listened to conversations going on around him. Only able to distinguish a word here and there, he gave up trying. Rather impatiently, he voiced, "Isn't there anyone in Paris who speaks English? I need Deb. She is the one who knows French. That is why she was assigned to me. Where is she?" He came upon an aristocratic building with a country flair. Above the door, inscribed in a very sophisticated script, were the words, 'The Palais Bourbon House.' Looking at the twelve massive columns boasting a distinctive appeal across the front of the building, his eyes rested on the words that were boldly accented above the ornate wood work of the columns, 'CORPS LEGISLATE.' Towering above and adding to the grandeur of the building was a tri-colored flag featuring vertical bands of red, white and blue. Malachi stood in reverence, momentarily, to the National Emblem of France.

Entering the government building, he was surprised when a middled aged lady approached him speaking very fluent English although with an accent. "May I help you?"

"Wow! You speak English!"

The lady smiled. "Yes, I do. I am Rina. What can I help you with?"

"I am here to see the United States Minister to France."

"Oh. You want Mr. Elihu Washburn. Follow me, please."

Following a few paces behind the very distinguished lady, Malachi smiled as the sound of her high heeled shoes echoed throughout the entrance hall and drowned out his own footsteps. Presently they stopped outside a door. After a soft knock, Rina opened it and preceded Malachi inside a very spacious, orderly room.

"Mr. Washburn, Malachi Hebron to see you."

Malachi looked in wonderment at the lady who had just escorted him into the Minister's office. *She knows who I am. I didn't give her my name.* His eyes followed her as she exited the room and closed the door behind her.

"Malachi, welcome to a part of the United States of America in Paris, France."

His thoughts interrupted, although still pondering how this lady knew his name, he turned to face a very unpretentious gentleman.

Minster Washburn greeted him with a friendly smile and handshake. "Why the worried frown, Malachi?"

"So many people seem to know me and know why I am in France, but I haven't the faintest idea who any of them are."

"All in the carefully laid out plan. Your mission didn't start when you boarded the SS Atlantic. It has been meticulously in operation long before that. You are the one chosen from several names as the Diplomatic Courier for this assignment. Now, let's see what we have."

Malachi removed the key from the mini pocket hidden beneath his belt. He unlocked the handcuff attached to his arm and put the attaché case on the Minister's desk. After removing the ring of the cuff from his arm and placing it beside the case, he handed the small key to Mr. Washburn. "The honor is yours, Sir."

"Have a seat, Malachi." The Minister continued to stand and opened the attaché case, slowly removing its contents. Easing down into a chair behind the desk, he held up a single sheet of paper.

A bit bewildered, Malachi asked, "Is that all that is in there? You mean I was plunged into the English Channel with that thing handcuffed to my arm and all it contains is one little sheet of paper?"

Mr. Washburn smile. "That you did. It is not the quantity but the quality that is important."

"Kind of like, it's not the packaging but what is inside that matters."

The Minister smile. "Exactly. Now, let's get down to the matter."

Malachi observed quietly as the head of American Affairs in France concentrated on the contents of the paper before him.

"So, you were sent to Paris to disclose the name of the man associated with the Credit Mobilier Scandal. Do you know who he is?"

"I do not, Sir. I do not know the man or his name. I only know as a Diplomatic Courier from the United States, I had to deliver this attaché case to you personally."

Mr. Washburn looked at Malachi. "The man is Louis de Berger. That doesn't surprise me. I am glad it isn't Baron Haussman."

"Who is Baron Haussman?"

"He is the man appointed to oversee a Paris reconstruction program. Haussman has been labeled a most extraordinary man, vigorous with many talents. Yet, I find him to be clever and devious if the need arises. Thus far he has been loyal to France, even after Napolean was ousted. Frankly, I like the man."

"So, Louis de Berger is the man we are after. Who is he? What did he do?"

"You don't know that, either?"

"No sir. I carried his name all the way across the Atlantic Ocean and had no clue. However, there were some who obviously knew. More than once there was an attempt on my life. Also my assistant, who was aboard the SS Atlantic, was exposed to grave danger. No one was supposed to know that we were acquainted much less working together, but, again, someone knew." Malachi hesitated before very bluntly asking, "By the way, where is my assistant? Our purpose for being sent here is to work together on this. I have not seen or heard from her since before I was plunged into the English Channel."

"First things, first. Now.."

Malachi stood to his feet. "Sorry to interrupt, Mr. Washburn. But where is Deborah Dotson? When and where will we meet? I am tired of being in the dark about everything, yet everybody seems to know me and my mission. I am concerned about Deborah."

Mr. Washburn stepped from behind his desk and laid a hand on Malachi's shoulder. "No, not everybody. Take it easy, son. As I said, first things, first. And the first thing is, you need to know about Louis de Berger. Now, sit back down."

Malachi ran his fingers through his hair, sat down and took a deep breath. He listened intently as his superior spoke.

"Louis de Berger, the man that you are to help apprehend, is a Frenchman. He posed as a representative of the United States and worked with the leaders of the Credit Mobilier Affair, which was a fraud, by collecting savings from French investors. He and his cohort in America, Thomas Durant, who was head of the Union Pacific Construction at the time, combined their lending schemes to further illegal usage of railroad money. This letter explains that. I have known the man to be dishonest, and, might I add, very dangerous."

"Minister, if I understand you correctly, France and America want Mr. Berger."

"That is correct. France wants him for stealing from his own people, while America wants him as a witness against Durant. The Credit Mobilier Affair is an example of the corrupt practices that characterized the period of the American Civil War."

"I will do my best to locate the man and help to apprehend him, but first, I must meet up with Deborah. Surely you know where she is."

Silence prevailed as Mr. Washburn took a sheet of paper from the desk drawer and removed the quill from the ink well. Malachi stared at the man. "Where.."

Washburn held up his hand as a signal for Malachi to hush. Obeying, Malachi endeavored to shake off the willies that had invaded his nervous system and watched the man write. When Washburn put down the quill and tore to pieces the paper that he had risked his life to bring from Washington D.C. to Paris, France, Malachi jumped to his feet with mouth agape.

The Minister looked up at him. "Sit down, Malachi."

Easing himself back down in the chair, Malachi accepted the paper from Mr. Washburn. "Here are your new instructions telling you where to go and what to do from this point. Memorize and then destroy them. As you move forward there must be no paper trails. Stop worrying about Deborah. Very soon you will see that she is well." The Minister stood to his feet and Malachi followed suit. "One last piece of advice. The man you are after is very sinister and conniving. He, no doubt, will set a trap for you, but you have the audacity and wit to counteract his trap with a more clever one."

Chapter 30

Malachi stepped out of the Embassy and took a deep breath of fresh air. Ushered down the street by anticipation and excitement, he whispered, "At last I am going to see Deborah. Together we will find this man and soon be on our way home to America and Bethel." Smiling, he repeated, "Yes, to Bethel, my safe place." Ignoring the wave of homesickness that washed over him and pushing aside the yearning for home, he allowed Mr. Washburn's parting words to fill his mind. *The man is sinister and conniving. He, no doubt, will set a trap for you, but you have the audacity and wit to counteract his trap with a more clever one.*

"You had better watch out Mr. Louis de Berger. You are about to have a hound dog and his assistant on your trail." A short distance from the Embassy, he turned the corner onto a side street. Wanting to run, he held his speed in check so as not to arouse suspicion from passersby. Settling for just a little pep in his walk, while paying no attention to what others were doing, he rounded another corner and turned onto a narrow street lined with buildings. On the opposite side was a row of trees accenting a beautiful river. Knowing it was the famous Seine River, he wished for time to sit on the bank and let the serenity of the peaceful flowing water absorb his whole being.

Looking again at the line of buildings, his eyes focused on one in particular. "Aha, there it is." With a set mind and determination he hurried straight for a brick building, rectangular in shape, very extravagant in color, and elaborately decorative. Stopping a few feet from the building, he studied the diagonal motifs that accented the exterior. Not only did the motifs add a special type of beauty, but Malachi knew they were also advantageous to the structure. Made of iron that was camouflaged by design and color, they helped the building to remain secure against hard winds that often swept through the city. "Very provocative," he uttered. "Like an anchor, they are holding the structure together. Not visible to the human eye, yet the building would crumble without them."

Making no attempt to try and pronounce the words scrawled across the front, Malachi stepped inside the building. He could not prevent the, "Wow," that escaped his lips. There were rows and rows of chocolate. Shelves that held chocolate squares and chocolate triangles, round chocolate and long slender chocolate. There were decorative wrapped chocolates enclosed by glass. Large potbellied jars filled with chocolate decorated the top of a counter. Very impressed, he said, "Never have I seen so much chocolate! It is obvious that I have just entered a chocolate factory!"

The place had seemed deserted when he walked in so he was surprised to hear a voice. He looked up as an elderly man approached rattling off words in French. When Malachi did not respond, the man said in broken English, "Ah.. American. Vous (you)..buy..some.. cho..co..late?"

"Well, maybe. I have never seen so much chocolate."

"Vous..like..bit..ter or sweet?"

"Sweet. Very sweet."

"Well..vous look." The old man walked behind the glass counter, turned his back and pretentiously appeared busy.

Malachi leaned on the counter. Understanding dawned. Bravely he asked, "Do you have bittersweet?"

The man spun around as fast as a spinning top. "Aha.. bit..ter..sweet." He moved from behind the counter and headed toward a closed door. It was evident he was walking better and faster than he had earlier.

Malachi proceeded to follow him, wondering if the man was really as old as he appeared at first sight.

THE ANCHOR

The man held up his hand and spoke in broken English. "No.. follow. Vous.. stay." Soon the man returned and handed Malachi a note, uttering two words. "Now go."

Another note. Always a note. Malachi hesitated at the door. He did not want to leave the building without seeing Deborah. *I was supposed to meet her here.* His thoughts were interrupted by a voice speaking perfect English. He turned as the old man approached.

"Surprised, are you, Malachi?"

Malachi shook his head. "Nothing surprises me anymore."

The man put his hand on Malachi's shoulder. "I am Arlo Pereire, proprietor of this establishment. Read the note. Remember, things and people are not always what they seem."

The street had become a busy hub. Looking around, he noted everyone seemed preoccupied with their own lives. Of course, with his little knowledge of the French language, if others were talking about him, he wouldn't know. He read the note in an almost inaudible voice. "Wait for me by the big clock near the bridge that crosses the Seine River. Deborah." Putting the note in the small inside slit of his jacket, he felt a slight bulge in his shirt. The small pistol in the pocket gave him some satisfaction of protection should he be set upon by some unexpected force and violence.

With one foot propped up, Malachi leaned against a lamp post near the river. He stared out across the Seine, listening to the ticking sound coming from the nearby clock. Out of his peripheral vision, he knew his presence drew a few stares, but most people simply ignored the fact that he was slouching against the post. Frequently, he looked toward the chocolate factory hoping to see Deborah walking toward him. Minutes ticked away. The hustle and bustle of the busy street dwindled down to almost desertion as shoppers headed home and merchants locked up their shops. The ticktocking of the clock became louder. He whispered, "I wonder where Deb is. It is getting late."

As evening shadows slowly made their way up the Seine River, Malachi, in spite of his anxiety, was awed by the pinky Parisan sky as the sun sank lower and lower behind the Paris skyline. "Maybe one day, Deb, you and I can sit on the docks of this river at evening time and enjoy this beauty together." Pushing such thoughts from his mind, he turned and was about to walk to the factory when suddenly something appeared from the opposite direction that brought him to a halt. The setting sun cast a long shadow down the street revealing a distorted outline of someone. Not knowing if the shadow belonged to a man or woman, it moved Malachi into action. He quickly moved toward the factory weaving in and out among the trees that lined the street, hesitating only long enough to determine if the shadow had disappeared or if it was moving his direction. Yes. It seemed to be following him.

Then he saw her. "Deborah! Stay there!" She lurked back into the darkness beside the building. Without another backward glance, he hastened and covered the distance between them. Grabbing her hand, words seemed to gush from him. "Run, Deborah Dotson, run for your life."

"Where to?" She asked as they ran. "I recall you telling me those same words back in Pueblo. That seems like an eternity ago instead of a few months. What are we running from and where are we running to?"

"I don't know where to. Just anywhere away from here." About that time a gunshot blasted and a bullet went whizzing into the atmosphere. "That is what we are running from. I don't know what it hit, but we are still on our feet." Quickly they rounded the corner of a side street and stepped onto a narrow path wedged between two buildings.

Completely exhausted, Deborah collapsed in his arms. "Malachi, I wondered if I would ever see you again."

Malachi held her close. "Now, now. I know."

"Here we are in a foreign country where people are still trying to repair damages from a war. I know the Germans are very unhappy and rebellion lurks ready to pounce on the loyal French people. But we were not part of that. What do they want with us? Who would want to shoot at us?"

"We will discuss it later. Right now I must get you to safety. Where are you staying?"

"At the Hotel d' Alsace."

Malachi peered around the corner of the building. No shadow, no noise. No movement. He whispered, "Maybe our would be assassin decided to wait for a better time. Let's get you inside a building where there are other people about. I saw the hotel earlier. It is at the far end of the same street as the Embassy." He took her hand. "You will have to walk behind me." They made their way down an alley barely wide enough for one to pass. Deborah followed close, clutching tightly to Malachi's hand.

Chapter 31

Weaving in and out among the many tables occupying the outdoor bistro, which was one of the most charming and social graces of Paris, Malachi led Deborah to a small two seater on the outskirts of the popular café. While wanting to stay close to a crowd for safety purposes, yet needing some privacy to be able to talk, he felt being right in the hub of things was as safe a place as any. Although crowded with Parisians and tourist, everyone was occupied with their own business at hand and did not seem at all interested in what others were saying or doing. Malachi took a big swallow of the refreshing drink from the seidel, a large thick glass of German origin. Designed for intoxicating drinks, the French decided a seidel was perfect for keeping cool the popular lemon flavored drink.

Malachi swallowed a big gulp. "Very tasty and good, but it does not come close to Zip's delicious lemonade. The French call it by some fancy name, but it is nothing more than lemon juice, water and sugar. I will be so glad to get back to America where lemonade is called lemonade and not citron something or other." He pointed to a sign advertising the drink. "Can you pronounce that, Deb?"

Ignoring the sign, Deborah looked instead at the small time piece pinned to her blouse. With elbows on the table and chin resting in the cup of her hands, she stared at Malachi. "Will you please quit stalling and tell me why I am in Paris, France. We have been at this table over twenty minutes and you keep avoiding the subject. I have to get back to the factory soon."

"Do you know anything at all about why you are here? What the assignment is?"

"All I know is that I was to report to Mr. Washburn at the Embassy. Which I did. He was to have my job at the chocolate factory arranged and also my accommodations. Which he did."

Malachi put the seidel down, reached across the table and touched Deborah's cheek with his hand. Then he took her small hand and held it up to his face. "I love you, Deborah Dotson."

"I love you, Malachi, but we still have a job to do. Tell me what I am supposed to do."

He took both her hands in his and rested their arms on the table. "You are like a rare wonderful dream. But more times than not, rare things have a way of vanishing. I don't want anything to happen to you."

"Nothing is going to happen to me."

"If only I could be sure of that."

"Malachi, there is only one thing in this world that we can be sure of, and that is, God remains the same. He keeps His Word. He has promised to be a shield, a fortress, a high tower. The Name of Jesus is a strong tower. A safe place."

"But…" Malachi squeezed her hands. "You are taking such a risk. It is dangerous."

She dared not remove her hands, although he was squeezing them to the point of pain. "That is where trust comes in. We were never promised smooth sailing. We have no assurance that we would never be forced to flounder about in troubled waters. As you well know."

"Yes, literally." He forced a grinned. "Troubled for sure, but I am afraid we are about to dive into turbulent waters. What would I do without you."

If you do not stop crushing my hands, I am not going to be much help. Refraining from voicing her thoughts, she smiled. "I am with you through thick and thin. Through peaceful waters or turbulent waves. So stop worrying."

Malachi released a big sigh. "Since your employment at the factory have you come in contact with a man called Louis de Berger or ever heard the name?"

Deborah leaned forward, her eyes bulging. "Yes," she whispered. "I have heard his name often. It seems some of the employees are always talking about him. I have never met him, but they say he comes in the factory frequently and buys the most expensive chocolates. The workers whisper among themselves. They say he is very rich. Wealth gotten by ill gains, from what I have gathered. The way they talk he is disliked by most all of France, especially in Paris. Yet, people cater to him. Coworkers say he is somebody to be feared."

"No doubt that is because he is so rich which tends to make him appear powerful. Have you heard if he has a bodyguard?"

"From what I have heard, he is always alone. However, Dinah, a lady I work closely with sometimes, said there are usually two men following him everywhere he goes. Although she personally has never seen them, other workers at the factory said they have seen the man in question at places other than the factory. Without fail, there are two men keeping a distance away so it won't be obvious that he has gunmen protecting him."

"That is a very pertinent piece of information. You are doing your job."

Deborah smiled. "My job also is to be your interpreter since you do not speak or understand French. But, I can't very well do that if I am not with you. Now can I?"

"We will be together as much as possible from now on."

"Dinah and others at the factory say the man doesn't want it known that he depends on anyone or anything for protection. He is a conniving, egotistical, rich scoundrel. Everywhere he goes he carries a fabricated air of power and strength."

Malachi released a soft chuckle and whispered, "Always remember the saying, nothing falls harder than a self-made tower of strength." He squeezed Deborah's hands again and gave her a teasing but reassuring grin. "Mr. Berger, you better look out. When Malachi Hebron and Deborah Dotson get through with you, your empire will have crumbled leaving only a big mess of nothing splattered on the grounds of France."

"The sooner the better." Realizing he had lessened his grip, Deborah slipped her hands from his and stood. "I must get back to the factory."

Escorting her to the factory, Malachi felt prickles crawling up and down his spine as they walked. It was as if eyes were boring into his backside. Not wanting to alarm Deborah, he muzzled his thoughts. *I know there is someone lurking in the shadows. I know someone is following us. Whoever it is doesn't want me to suspect anything. Well, I have news for him. I don't have to see him to know he is there.* Touching the pistol that rested securely inside his shirt pocket, he hastened his steps.

"What is it, Malachi?" Deborah asked as she quickened her pace to match his.

"Oh, it's nothing. Just want to get you to the factory so you can tune in to any bit of information about Berger." With eyes and ears alert and ready should any action come from the person dogging their trail, his effort to focus on what Deborah was saying was fruitless.

"Malachi Hebron," Deborah said with a slight rise in her voice. "You have not heard a word that I have said."

"Sorry, Deb. What did you say?"

"I asked why no one in France uses the passcode? I don't know who can be trusted."

"Remember the warning, trust no one."

"But Mr. Washburn didn't use it. He didn't seem to know it. When I asked for the passcode, he gave me a strange look and said, what passcode."

"They don't use the passcode in France. It is more like an identifying phrase or question. Your boss hum hauled around about what kind of chocolate I like until I asked if he had bittersweet."

"Oh. Nothing was said about bittersweet to me."

"It wasn't necessary. Mr. Washburn had everything arranged for you." Malachi trembled from another round of prickles along his spine. Arriving at the chocolate factory, he stopped outside the door and looked up and down the street.

Deborah took hold of his arm. "What is wrong? Tell me, Malachi."

"We are being followed. Don't be alarmed. Just act normal and stay alert and cautious. I will be here when you get off work to walk you back to the hotel. Do not leave the factory if I am not here. Wait inside for me." Opening the door, he followed Deborah inside the factory, middling around momentarily. Satisfied that whoever was on their trail was not going to follow them inside, he left the building and ambled nonchalantly down the street. Picking up a crumbled piece of paper, he wadded it into a ball and tossed it up in the air while turning around and proceeding down the street backward, all the while keeping an eye on the factory entrance. Thoughts hurled through his mind like a cannonball. *It doesn't matter how indispensable you think you are and how intimidating you are to others, Mr. Berger. You may be the best at what you do but even the best have their flaws. You have your hunters on my trail, dogging my every step, while you sit back and laugh, waiting for me to be caught in your trap.* Malachi stopped as his thoughts became verbal. "But I have news for you, often the first victim caught in a trap is the reckless hunter who set it. So beware, you are destined to be caught in the snare that you have prepared for me. And that's a fact!"

Chapter 32

After leaving Deborah at the chocolate factory and confident that Mr. Pereire would see to her safety while she was at work, Malachi hastened down the street, turned the corner and in a hurry scurry headed to the Embassy. He needed to have a talk with Mr. Elihu Washburn and quick. Arriving at the building and taking the steps two at a time, he rushed through the door and came face to face with the sophisticated lady who had met him the first time he entered the Embassy.

"Welcome, Malachi. How can I help you?"

Malachi did not miss the swift look of surprise that flashed across her face and set off his brain alarm system. Nevertheless, very calmly he replied, "Rina, I need to see Mr. Washburn, please."

"But… he isn't in. I thought…oh, well."

"Can you tell me where he is? It is urgent that I speak with him."

"I thought you two were together." Seeing the questioning look on Malachi's face, she continued. "Mr. Washburn left about an hour ago. He said he had an errand to run and afterwards he was going to locate you."

"I haven't seen him. Maybe we missed each other in transit."

"I am sorry but that is all he told me, Malachi." The worried frown on his countenance let Rina know he was deeply concerned. "No need to be alarmed. Since, obviously, he hasn't seen you, I expect he will be back here soon."

Malachi uttered a brief thank you and hastened out of the Embassy. *Mr. Washburn must have some new and pertinent information. Well, he is searching for me and I am searching for him. Maybe we will cross paths.* Walking away from the building, he voiced, "We need to communicate better. I wonder if he went to see Deb?" He turned a corner going in the opposite direction from the street that would have taken him to the factory. "Well, whatever you want with me, Mr. Elihu Washburn, will have to wait as well as my business with you, unless we end up at the same place. I must get to the bank." Not familiar with that particular street, at the moment he wished he could be two places at once. He released a short chuckle. "Oh if only it were possible to call into existence Anna's little game of 'me, myself and I' in which she pretended to be three people when I refused to play house with her. I've been through some things since then. Some good and some bad." Assaulted by a wave of nostalgia, he stopped in his tracks. "Just to be home for a short time. To feel the warmth and security of Bethel. A Stronghold! An Anchor! Papa, Momma, Zip, everybody, I miss all of you so much!"

Arriving at The Credit Mobilier Bank of Paris, Malachi paused outside the door for a moment to refresh his memory of the briefing he had received about the financial failure of the institution. The bank was owned and operated by two brothers of Portuguese Jewish descent, Emile and Isaac Pereire, and under their wise supervision had flourished very well for several years. He was also advised that the brothers had recently closed the bank due to misappropriations of funds and bad investments, and the man he was to apprehend was largely responsible for the financial collapse. With his debonair but devious ways, the corrupt man had earned the brothers trust and by manipulation and bribery of others had practically swindled the thriving business to bankruptcy. All of France knew the Pereire Brothers came from a long line of wealthy business men who were very knowledgeable in financial affairs. So it was a shocking surprise when the bank closed its doors. Even those who did not patronize their bank would quickly admit to the brothers diligence and trustworthiness. Arlo Pereire, owner of the chocolate factory and a cousin to Emile and Isaac, readily concurred to that fact.

Malachi took a deep breath and reached for the door handle. To his surprise the door was locked. Knowing one of the Pereire brothers was supposed to meet him, he gave three loud knocks and waited. The door opened momentarily and Malachi found himself face to face with, although slightly overweight, a very stately looking gentleman.

"Mr. uh..Pereire?"

"Maybe. Who wants to know?"

Malachi stepped forward. "I'm…" The man inside gave him a slight shove and closed the door in his face. Immediately it opened again. The man's whole frame covered the opening. Although tempted to return the shove, Malachi decided against it considering the fact he would no doubt bounce back like a rubber ball attacking a brick wall.

The man spoke in a business but skeptical tone. "Is there something you want? The bank is no longer doing business. What are you doing here?"

Malachi cleared his throat. "I am Malachi Hebron."

"So."

"According to Mr. Washburn, I am supposed to meet a Mr. Pereire."

"So. Washburn. Hebron. Names mean nothing to me."

Impatiently, Malachi looked up and down the street. He then placed one hand on the door and the other against the frame, bracing himself for any unwelcome backlash. Halfway expecting the man inside to give him a punch in the face or a poke in the stomach along with another shove, he tried desperately to hide the intimidation brought on by the large bulk that loomed before him. When the man did nothing but stare, feeling a bit of self-confidence steal its way into his mind, Malachi endeavored to speak in a low but precise voice. "I know the Credit Mobilier Bank was always known for its great French flair and prestige. By no means, do I intend to discredit that."

"So."

Malachi felt his recently acquired self-confidence seeping away like a grain of sand carried with the tide. *Here is a man of few words, or so it appears. I don't know if he is friend or foe.* Unsure if the timing was right for him to ask the question that was on the tip of his tongue and would tell the tale, yet he was running out of patience with this unmovable stone standing before him. With a hard swallow, he downed the saliva that had accumulated in his mouth and leaned his head slightly toward the man. Mustering up enough gumption to speak, he did so in a subdued voice. "Since the bank is closed for business," Malachi lowered his tone to barely a whisper. "I was wondering, do you have any wooden nickels?"

The man opened his mouth but before even one syllable escaped, quickly clamped it shut again. Malachi was aware of the incredulous expression that flashed across the stoic countenance. Neither did he miss the twitch of the nose nor the flick of the eye lash, before a strong hand grabbed his arm and jerked him inside. The man closed the door and bolted it, never releasing his firm grip on Malachi's arm. Wanting to jerk his arm free but anticipating that he may have to spend the rest of his life with only one arm, he wisely considered the situation. Deciding to try and free himself from the iron clutch that held him captive was not a good choice, he resisted the urge. Still pondering if he was with foe or friend and hoping it was the latter, he tried to relax. A pounding on the door caused him to jerk and endeavor to take a backward look but brought no reaction whatever from his companion. As the man ushered him down a narrow hallway, several more vigorous poundings vibrated the atmosphere. The walls surrounding the two seemed to quake before the poundings gradually faded and silence prevailed.

Still propelled by the clench of the strong hand, Malachi ventured a plea. "Will you please release your hold on me, sir? That arm has served me well and is very valuable. Your vise grip is unnecessary, I can assure you. And another thing, if you do not let go, that precious limb is going to be like a misplaced participle dangling from the rest of my body."

Malachi's attempt at wry humor was rebuffed by a scowl as the man stopped at a room entrance. After shoving him through the doorway and keeping a firm hold on his arm, the man followed him into the room, closed the door and engaged the bolt lock. Only then did he release his grip and point to a chair. "You are just another young whippersnapper who seems to think he is invincible even when he knows that danger lurks down every street and around every corner. Sit down, Malachi Hebron."

Rubbing his arm and giving the man a quizzical look, Malachi wasn't sure which surprised him most. The man speaking or the smile that creased his countenance.

"I am Emile Pereire. Don't worry, you are not going to be bothered with a dangling participle."

Malachi rubbed his arm again and gave Mr. Pereire a lopsided grin. "Wish I could be as sure about that as you are. Why did you jerk me inside so quickly?"

"Why did you wait so long to give the identifying question?"

"Well, uh… just trying to keep my ducks in order."

Mr. Pereire harrumphed. "Ducks in order? Young man you were a sitting duck in line of the hunters beam."

"Sir? You saw him?"

"To your advantage a sun ray fell across the barrel of a gun. The sparkling reflection caught my eye. You can thank Jehovah God for that."

With bowed head and without reservation Malachi quoted from Psalm 46. "God is our refuge and strength. A very present help in trouble. Therefore will not we fear…"

For a few moments both men were silent. Malachi looked up as Mr. Pereire spoke. "Is that the God you serve, Malachi?"

"That is the God I serve, Mr. Pereire."

"Well, you better hold Him to that promise for you have arrived headlong and headstrong right into the midst of trouble. You are going to need more help than any human can give. That's for sure and for certain."

Chapter 33

Longing for sleep, Deborah lay on the bed in the pitch blackness of the night. With eyes wide open, she endeavored to push aside the many voices that were having a heyday in her brain. Her efforts were in vain. Trying to dispel a frightening, uncanny feeling that the light quilt pulled up to her chin was slowly disintegrating, she grabbed it with both hands just to be sure. Clutching it tightly, she refused to loosen her hold yet the feeling of it disappearing remained. In its place, she felt the quietness and stillness of the eerie darkness creep its way from her feet to her head until completely covering her like a shroud. As her vivid imagination began to run wild, the voices in her head got fainter and fainter. Feeling a bit drowsy, she closed her eyes and welcomed the slumber that had eluded her earlier, hoping that when she awoke, her mind would be unmuffled and things would be clearer. However, what she thought would be a refreshing, peaceful sleep was anything but that.

She fell into a fitful dream. *Someone was chasing her. She could see the outline of a man but his face was a blur. She had been running for days. There was no place to hide. Exhausted and heaving for breath, she ran on, sometimes stumbling but always managing to regain her balance and press forward. She ran over rocky steeps and dashed through quiet springs. She ran in sand along the banks of turbulent waters. She saw a helpless vessel tossing on angry waves and then suddenly there appeared a line going down from the little ship to a solid rock. She kept running, but the vessel stayed within her peripheral vision. It was weaving on the surface of the water yet still remained secured underneath by something stronger and mightier than the little vessel. The painting at home jumped into her very soul and before her eyes, but the words were fuzzy and indiscernible. She kept running and running. In the distance a big rock appeared on the sandy shore. Weak and stumbling in the sand, she kept whispering, just a little farther. Just a little farther. Pressing her way onward, she stretched her arm toward the rock. Running and stretching and reaching, yet it remained just beyond her grasp. She was moving but did not seem to be gaining ground. Then there it was, right in front of her. Exhausted, she ducked behind the big rock. Leaning against it, she eased herself to a sitting position and breathed easier, feeling a sense of security in its shelter. She had to think. She had to get a grip on her emotions and actions. To her dismay, the rock disappeared just as quickly as it came leaving her bared and desolate. She heard a noise beside her but no one was there. The man who was chasing her earlier had vanished. With her hand balled into a fist, hoping to quiet the invisible person or thing beside her, she pounded into the sand. When the noise continued, agitated by the continuous clamor, she grabbed at it. This only resulted in creating a conglomeration of louder noises.*

The cacophony of sound that rang in her ears like a giant bell roused her from her dream world thrusting her back into the real world. Realizing it was the ringing alarm clock that she had been pounding and sent crashing onto the floor, Deborah got out of bed. Picking up the quilt and holding it up to her face, she sighed with relief that it was the real thing. *Of course, Deborah, it's the real thing. What did you expect.* She could not completely push aside the feeling of it disappearing. The words from the painting that were obscured in her dream were now clear in her mind. Speaking them aloud as she had many times over the past several months, their meaning impacted her greater than ever. "The Anchor holds in spite of the storm." Dressing quickly, she left the hotel and hastened down the street to the factory, starting her work day with one thought upper most in her mind. *I hope my day is not as terrifying as my night.*

"Are you okay, Deborah?"

Deborah turned her head and looked into the eyes of her coworker. She was completely unaware that Dinah had covered the distance between them and was standing beside her. Deborah gave her a questioning look knowing the work standard at the factory was to maintain three feet from the next worker, and Dinah was a stickler to the rules. Yet, having already discovered, if it became necessary, her friend would stretch the rules a bit.

"I am all right. Is anything wrong?" Leaning over she whispered in Dinah's ear. "Do you have news about Mr. Berger?"

"The question is, what is wrong with you?"

"Nothing. Why do you ask?"

"Because you have been standing there staring into space for at least ten minutes. And besides that, you have wrapped and unwrapped that same square of chocolate umpteen times. What is bugging you?"

"As I said, nothing."

Dinah gave her a doubtful look. "I did hear that Berger wants to hire a young woman to assist his head housekeeper. Why are you so anxious for news of him?" Dinah put her hand on Deborah's shoulder. "Hey, you are not interested in that guy, are you? Why, Deborah, the man is old enough to be your father. He may be rich, but you surely do not want to get involved with the likes of him." Dinah moved her face a little closer to Deborah and gave her a scrutinizing stare. "Oh no."

Deborah smiled. "It is not what you think." Noticing the other workers were casting frowning looks their direction, she said, "We are drawing attention, so let's get back to work. Thanks for being my friend, Dinah, and for interrupting by reverie." She lowered her voice to a whisper. "If you do hear something about this notorious character, please tell me."

Dinah patted Deborah's arm. She walked away from the younger woman with a worried and puzzled look creasing her brow. Disturbing thoughts beset her. *I wonder why Deborah is always asking about Berger. She doesn't seem to know him. Yet, I have noticed how her attention perks when someone mentions his name. Come to think of it, more often than not she is prodding or prompting somebody for information. How in the world could someone like Deborah Dotson be involved with such an unscrupulous, devious human. If he is human. The things I have heard about him gives a person reason for doubt.*

Resuming her duty, Deborah occupied her fingers with wrapping chocolate. However, mentally that was not the case. Her brain refused to wrap around such a menial task when there were so many more important things pressing her. She had heard nothing worthwhile about Berger in a week. He had not been in the factory since her employment two weeks ago. The only thing she had gleaned, other than Dinah relating he wants to hire a young woman to assist the housekeeper, was due to her overhearing a conversation between two of the workers. They were informed the man was out of circulation and refused to see anyone other than his housekeeper and valet. Those two seldom left the Villa, sending a lackey to take care of basic tasks and run errands. Added to her frustration was that terrifying dream. Try as she might she could not force herself to dismiss the fact that maybe it was a warning of imminent danger.

I feel like Mawmaw's pressure cooker that has built up too much steam and is about to blow its top. If I don't hear something or do something soon, my pressure valve is bound to explode. She stood there trying to wrap chocolate while all the time wrapped around her brain was the reality that soon and very soon she and Malachi must someway get positive information of Berger's actions. *Somewhere there are papers that we have to confiscate before the man can be brought in for questioning and arrest. But, I cannot do anything without Malachi.* Holding an unwrapped piece of chocolate in midair, she had a sudden inspiration. *Or can I? With a little subterfuge and wit, it is possible I may expose him and his shams.* Just as a scheme began to form in her mind, the sudden impact of a voice blew her idea to smithereens. Giving in to an overwhelming power of hysterics, she released a piercing cry. In a state of delirium, she stood with clenched fists and gave way to a screaming fit. She felt hands on her shoulders. Somebody was shaking her very hard which only made her scream louder. Someone was talking. At first it was like an echo then the voice seemed to get closer and clearer.

"Deborah. Deborah. Snap out of it." The voice was not loud but rang with authority. "Stop screaming."

But Deborah did not want to stop screaming. It felt good to scream after months of running and hiding. Spending weeks on a ship. Sailing through a raging wind storm. Trampling over dead people and watching helplessly as some wretched person threw Malachi into the English Channel. She felt like a scream or two was her due. The pressure inside her had finally reached its limit and like the pressure cooker, her top blew off. She wanted to keep screaming until this nightmare was over.

Dinah saw the good shaking she was giving the girl was not affecting the hysterical outburst. She also knew there was only one sure way to stop it. *I hate to do this to you.* With that thought she gave Deborah a gentle slap across the face. Dinah hesitated as the screaming continued. *Okay. Here goes.* This time it was not a gentle but a hard slap. Then she wrapped both arms around the screaming, trembling girl and held her in that embrace until the screaming hushed and the trembling subsided.

Chapter 34

Removing a stool from a corner of the room where Mr. Emile Pereire had led him, or to be exact had forced him to enter, Malachi smiled remembering the firm grip of the man. *I wasn't sure if he was friend or foe. He seemed so forceful and stern. Yet, he was actually gentle and kind. I have no doubt but what he could be frightful if a situation presented itself. Sure am glad he was on my side.* The two men had spent hours going through files and scrutinizing bank records to get all available information about Louis de Berger and his involvement with the Credit Mobilier Scandal of America. While coming across several business transactions the man had with the bank, none of them pointed to illegal deeds. They hoped to find substantial evidence of criminal acts and his misuse of the famous bank name as a cover up.

Due to a prior engagement, Mr. Pereire left the building instructing Malachi to stay as long as was needful but to use the back exit when leaving and be sure to lock the door. Anxious to find some pertinent proof among back records of the bank, Malachi did not want to stop in midstream to meet Deborah at the chocolate factory. Scribbling a short note, he asked Mr. Pereire to see that she got it.

Standing on the stool and looking upward, the particular drawer that drew his interest was, of course, at the very top of a filing cabinet. Stretching himself and balancing his carcass on tiptoes, he managed to put his hand inside the drawer that was labeled 'dead file, for manager's eyes only.' Thinking that all the files are dead since the bank is closed, and Mr. Pereire did not name a particular one that was off limits, he removed several folders from the drawer and stepped off the stool. Hours passed as he diligently searched paper after paper. Reading until blurred vision and crossed eyes hindered his focus, he placed his elbows on the desk and rested his head on his hands.

Listening to the chiming of the clock that overlooked the Seine River and was a landmark of the city, he counted each resounding gong. "Oh my. Eight o'clock. Deborah and I usually meet at the dining hall. After visiting with her and eating a good meal, maybe I can get some much needed sleep." Hurriedly, he put papers back into folders then placed them in a neat pile on the floor beside the desk. He shut off the lantern, stepped outside and attempted to put the door key into the keyhole. A wham on the back of the head sent him toppling downward. His body recoiled with pain as he was pulled over the bumpy threshold of the door by a not too gentle strong hand that had hold of his arm with a mastery death grip. In a semi-conscious state he could hear his own stuttering voice. "Oh..oh. Not another dan…gl..ing part..ti..ci..ple."

"What did he say?" The voice seemed to come from a distant land.

"Beats me what he was blubbering about." The reply was barely distinguishable. Words were like an echo as Malachi drifted into a state of incognizance.

Opening his eyes to complete darkness, he could not recall where he was and why his head was resting sideways on the top of a desk. The throbbing in his head at that moment brought him to an upright position. Vigorously, he massaged his temples trying to rid himself of the painful ache that was causing such physical distress and hindering his thinking ability. A vague awareness of his surroundings gradually began to penetrate the dullness of his senses. He needed some light. Forcing himself to stand, Malachi felt as if the room was circling around the desk. Clumsily, he grabbed hold of the edge for support. Steadying himself somewhat, he realized it was not a rotating room but a bout of dizziness that brought on a swooning. Pushing aside the unwanted feeling that was trying to overpower him, although still quite wobbly, he eased away from the desk. Managing to locate the lantern, he flipped it on. What was hidden in the darkness became vibrantly exposed as the luminous light filled the room. The desk that he had used for a pillow was littered with papers from one corner to the other. Empty folders lay scattered over the floor. Shutting his eyes tightly in a desperate struggle to remember what could have possibly brought on the untidy mess, his mind went back to when he stepped out of the bank. From that point, he drew a blank.

Who knows what occurred between then and until I came to with a pulsating pain that seems to be doing a stampede from the back to the forefront of my head. He failed to convince himself it was only his imagination. *Now I have imagined some pretty wild things in my short life, but to eradicate several hours of my evening is not possible. No way. But what happened? Something is causing this constant throbbing that refuses to ease. I am not imagining that.* Skeptically, he felt the back of his head. Sure enough, there was a lump.

Massaging his temples again he struggled to bring into focus all that had taken place over the past few hours. He heard the distant sound of a foghorn and the tolling of the bell from the chapel belfry. Listening to the familiar sounds the events of the day began to unfold. *Someone hit me then drug me back inside the building. From the mess this room is in, that person wants the same thing I do.* Giving the lump on his head another rub, he voiced, "And you are, also, responsible for this oversized goose egg that refuses to stop causing me pain. Whoever you are."

Not having any idea how long he had mentally and physically been out of sorts, Malachi counted the harmonious musical chimes of the clock as it announced the hour. On the stroke of midnight the tone of the timepiece seemed to move across the Seine River leaving a lingering assurance that time stops for no one. Like a jigsaw puzzle, pieces of his recent encounter with someone who definitely did not mean him well came together. Feeling like he had just received a hard punch in the stomach, he groan. "Deb. Oh, Deb, I did it again. I missed a second meeting with you. Please forgive me."

Due to the fact that the manager would not look kindly to a young man intruding upon the privacy of one of his guest after midnight, especially an unmarried female, he dismissed the thought of going to see Deborah at the hotel. Pondering whether to go to his own place of abode and still feeling the after effects of the bothersome goose egg on his head, which he hoped was not going to be a permanent fixture, he decided staying at the bank would probably be the safest place to spend the rest of the night. Hurrying over to the door and finding it still unlocked, he breathed a sigh of relief that his attackers had not decided to come back to use him again as a measuring stick for their strength.

Considering the mess the intruders had made and knowing things had to be put in order before Mr. Pereire arrived back at the bank, he busied himself with tidying up the place. After every piece of paper had been retrieved and the folders stacked neatly on the top of the desk, planning to put them back into the filing cabinet later, he sat down. He had to think. He must come up with a plan. There was so much going on, his brain seemed to be one big blur. His thoughts were obscure. Possibilities arose but they all seemed elusive and unreachable. In the midst of the confusion, without a warning Bethel appeared in his mind like a torch, and Papa paraphrasing the great English Poet, Robert Browning. The words burning in his heart erupted from his own voice like fire. "Malachi, a man's reach was designed to exceed his grasp. If what you are reaching for seems unattainable you try, and try, and stretch, and stretch yourself until at last you can grab hold. It may be only a slim thread at first grab but hold to it tenaciously until you have achieved what had seemed unachievable." At that moment, Papa's words impacted him greater than ever before. Knowing he must eventually extend his present reach, he kept groping for a clear path and a sensible solution.

Suddenly, in spite of the murky mess in his mind, an idea began to form. As if struck by a bolt of lightning, he stood. Like a bright light shining inside his brain, a plan suddenly became lucid. "It might work. Sensible, it is not. But…it is a solution. It just might work." He walked around the room, outlining every little detail of the plan in his mind. "First, I will have to okay it with Mr. Washburn. He may be a little hesitant but will give his approval. Then, I will tell Deb the plan. It will not be so easy persuading her. She will say it is too reckless, too risky and too dangerous. And it is. But somehow, she must be convinced."

Heedless to Malachi, who was so caught up in his own thoughts and satisfied that he had at last come up with a means to capture and bring to justice Mr. Berger, the chimes of the clock rang throughout the city announcing to all of Paris it was five o'clock and daylight was quickly approaching.

Chapter 35

"So where is your young man?" Dinah asked as she and Deborah walked from the chocolate factory to the hotel.

Deborah gave her a surprised look. "My young man?"

"Yes. The one that usually escorts you to the hotel?"

"How did you know that?"

"Deborah, I am not blind."

"But I thought …" her voice trailed off. "You…you always leave work before I do."

"Oh I've been around. I have seen you two together." Dinah gave her a searching look. "You thought? Mark my words, Deborah, more times than not our thoughts get us into trouble. Just because we think something is true does not mean that it is true. But… that is what we want to believe so we convince ourselves it is true. And might I add, do not believe everything you hear. More often than not an untruth is spread in an effort to conceal the truth. It doesn't matter who or how many are convinced to believe the false, it will not turn into truth. No matter how many times a falsehood is told and no matter how many so called honest people tell it, the truth remains the truth."

"That reminds me of what Mawmaw Dorcas would say when a bit of gossip started circling around Pueblo. Believe nothing you hear and only half of what you see." Arriving at the hotel entrance, Deborah grasped Dinah's hand. Sensing the woman's concern was genuine, the temptation to confide in her was strong, yet Deborah felt a restraint as the warning, *trust no one, trust no one*, sprinted over her brain. She made their parting simple but sincere. "Thank you for walking with me and for being my friend." After giving Dinah's hand a squeeze, she stepped into the hotel. Holding onto the banister and cautiously making her way up the stairs, she pondered what possible reason lay behind Dinah's concern. There were other times Malachi had not met her at the factory, but Dinah had shown no interest. Of course, she had never gone into a raging, screaming fit before. But still, Deborah could not wrap her mind around the fact that her outburst merited such a sudden shower of protection that she did not need and most definitely did not want.

In her room, she kicked off her shoes, climbed upon the bed and sat cross legged in the very center. She analyzed in her mind the situation. *Does Dinah know the real reason I am in Paris? Is she an undercover agent? If so, was she planted at the chocolate factory to help me or harm me? I wonder.* The longer she sat and tried to make some kind of logic of the whole business, the more questions arose to baffle her. Resting her head on her hands and taking a couple of deep breaths offered no solution for regaining her peace of mind. Realizing she was getting nowhere and accomplishing nothing, she removed her carcass from the bed. After such an unusual day at work, she decided freshening up at bit and changing her dress may possibly help her appearance, if not her feelings. Removing a magazine from the dresser, she went downstairs to wait for Malachi. The note from him that Mr. Pereire had slipped into her hand before leaving work was short and precise. It simply stated he would meet her later in the dining hall of the hotel but offered no explanation why he did not meet her at the factory.

An hour passed while she sat at a table twiddling her thumbs as her mind wrestled with the question that kept rolling over and over. *Where is he? Where is he?* For the second time, she thumbed through the magazine that displayed the latest in Paris fashions. Another hour passed and Malachi did not show. Sitting there unable to focus on anything, her imaginations were running wild. She glanced toward the entrance of the dining area and noticed the hotel proprietor was eyeing her. Feeling a bit uncomfortable under his glaring stare and assuming the man was ready to close the dining hall for the night, she stood and picked up her magazine. Casting a slight smile his direction, she made her exit.

Walking across the hotel lobby to the stairs, Deborah tried desperately to restrain the tears. Try as she might, still the watery drops oozed from her eyes and rolled down her cheeks. She no longer cared to hold them back but let them have free course and was totally unaware of the wet splotches that decorated her blouse as each tear dropped from her chin. Twice in one day Malachi did not show. She felt overwhelmed. She wanted to yell at him, at anybody. It didn't really matter at whom, she just wanted to yell. Rushing up the stairs, she clamped a hand over her mouth to prevent another screaming fit that was on the verge of erupting. Flinging herself across the bed, she buried her face in the pillow to muffle the moans and groans that had been inside her far too long. Completely consumed with an emotional outburst, time meant nothing.

Maybe it was the distant blowing of a train whistle, or the ringing of a bell echoing from the chapel belfry, or possibly the lonely sound of a foghorn that aroused her. Opening her eyes, she could not even remember when her emotions settled down from loud verbal hysterical noises to tossing and turning like a tumbleweed in a dust storm. Although able to force her body to stillness, the twisting of her insides remained. She felt as if she had been soaked in liquid, wrung out one way and then another until there was no dripping moisture, and then hung out to dry.

Chimes from the big clock that overshadowed the Seine River seemed to bounce off the water waves and flow into her room as if carried on the flapping wings of a soaring bird. She counted each gong as the big pendulum swung back and forth eventually sounding the hour letting all of Paris know that night would soon be history and the dawning of a new day was nearing. Waiting for the next musical sounds of the clock that would let her know another hour had passed, she remained still but anxious. Even though the chiming was silent until the clock struck the next hour, Deborah knew the pendulum was not still. With a continuous swing and without changing its speed, the amazing pendulum always took the same amount of time to make a complete swing, left to right then right to left and on and on. While trying to synchronize her timing with the movement of a pendulum, her mind was captivated by a somber reality. *Life is like that pendulum. Just as sure as the pendulum of the clock swings to the left, it will swing back to the right. Life's swing will take you into fear and sudden danger where hope and peace and safety seem out of reach. Then the pendulum of life will swing back again in the opposite direction where safety and peace and hope wait for you.*

Deborah sat up on the edge of the bed. A memory of childhood gripped her. *She was seven years old and had sneaked back downstairs after everyone retired for the night. She could hear voices. Whispering voices. Knowing they were coming from Pawpaw and Mawmaw Dotson's bedroom, she leaned her ear against the door. She heard Pawpaw Silas speaking soothing and comforting words.* "Maw, remember the Holy Scripture. 'This too shall pass.'"

The sound of the big clock brought her back to the present. "This too shall pass," she whispered. She did not count the gongs of the clock but as the last one sounded and vibrated into the distance, she knew another hour was forever gone. In her mind's eye she saw the pendulum of the clock of her life swinging back to the right. As her seemingly never ending, tumultuous night faded away like a slow moving fog drifting out to sea, the morning Deborah longed for finally dawned.

After her outburst at work, Arlo Pereire advised her not to go to the factory the next day but to stay in bed and rest, her body and her mind. Trying to will herself to do so only succeeded in making her more miserable. The semi-comfortable bed she had crawled into several hours earlier now felt prickly and scratchy. Relieved that she did not have to face the drudgery of wrapping chocolate and ignoring the scrutinizing stares of coworkers, yet she did not intend to stay in the hotel room and do nothing. Giving one last look into the mirror hanging above the bureau, she pinched her cheeks trying to force a little color into them while hoping to brighten her disheartened countenance. Although a lot of unanswered questions still loomed before her, top priority was Malachi. Locating him would solve her most pressing problem and rip away the drapery of despondency that clung to her like a deadly parasite. Clueless as to his whereabouts, nevertheless, with a set mind and determination that before this day ended they would be together, she left the hotel.

Wanting to see Mr. Washburn, however, before going to the Embassy, Deborah felt the need to rid herself of the jumbled up mess that was wreaking havoc in her mind. Making her way to the Seine River, she sat on the bench near the big clock. She had to think, think, think but with clarity and rationally. *Mr. Washburn is supposed to know where Malachi is every minute. That doesn't mean that he does, knowing Malachi the way I do. Or do I know him? I am not sure anymore. Maybe he has changed.* She refused to let herself dwell on that possibility. *Of course, you know him. He is the same Malachi. Witty and carefree, yet stable, dependable and true.* "And I love him," she whispered. "It's this job. It is so unpredictable. So mindboggling. But I will not let it conquer me."

Chapter 36

"Ridiculous! Preposterous!" Mr. Washburn pounded the desk with his hands.

With a lopsided grin, Malachi looked at his superior. He knew Mr. Washburn had not yet finished voicing denial of his plan. *Patience, Malachi, patience. Give him time to get over the first initial shock.*

"And wipe that grin off your face!"

Malachi swiped his hand across his face and sat with a solemn expression knowing there was more rebuff to come.

"Absurd! Unreasonable! Have you gone completely insane?"

The grin returned to his face as Malachi sat forward. *Do I dare venture to speak?*

As if reading his thoughts, Mr. Washburn said, "Don't say a word. I said wipe that grin off your face."

Malachi kept his mouth closed but his mind was far from quiet. *It will work. I know it will work. How to convince him of that is the problem.*

Mr. Washburn spun around and walked away from the desk. He knew something must be done to outwit Berger. The man had been questioned by him and French officials concerning the matter but had managed to come through the few inquiries clear as a whistle. Now, there was no doubt the man was blamable, although his guilt had yet to be proven. The Minister turned and faced Malachi. "Four years the man has been structing like a peacock all over Paris, gloating in his ability to deceive and manipulate. For nearly a year I have known the individual involved in the scandal was here but did not know his name." Mr. Washburn balled one hand into a fist and slammed it against the other. "All this time he has eluded the law."

Not intimidated by his actions or defeated by his outright refusal, Malachi spoke with confidence. "It will work, Minister. I know it will."

Elihu Washburn walked back to the desk. The tone of his voice had softened a bit, but there was still an evident *no* in his expression. "You do not know any such thing. What makes you so sure?"

"It is a good plan. I have faith."

"You have faith? Let me tell you something. You listen and you listen well. Sometimes we humans have misplaced faith. We tend to want to do something so strongly and conjure up enough gumption to risk it, but that doesn't constitute faith. More times than not, it is nothing but blind ignorance."

"Yes sir. But..but, it is a brilliant plan."

"Brilliant? It is outrageous! You are setting yourself up for the archer's arrow. You could lose your life. It is too risky, too dangerous."

"That goes with the job, Mr. Washburn."

Washburn gave him an unflinching stare. He liked the young man sitting before him. Adventurous and daring, yet there was an aura of stability and integrity about him that was rare among men. "You are teetering and tottering on the brink of annihilation! No job is that worthy, Malachi."

Beyond any doubt, his words spoke of refusal. However, a slight change in the man's countenance let Malachi know he may give his okay, if not his approval. Malachi stood. "Will you at least give more thought to my plan?"

Without replying, Mr. Washburn walked toward the door which was a clue for Malachi to leave. He had other things to do.

After closing the door behind him, Malachi opened it again just enough to poke his head inside the room. "It will work, Mr. Washburn. I know it will."

Looking through the window of his office, Washburn watched Malachi hasten down the street. "It probably will work, Malachi Hebron. With your courage and adamant nature, I honestly believe you could pull it off." Walking away from the window and shaking his head, he repeated. "It is ridiculous." He paced around the room. "Implausible. Illogical."

Returning to the window, his eyes roamed over nearby buildings and streets. Owners were opening their shops preparing for the day's business. Pedestrians hurried along, some tourist and others heading to their work places. With his mind wrapped around the young man and his idea to apprehend Berger, what was going on outside the building appeared as one hazy mist. Try as he might, he could not come up with one sensible reason for allowing such a risk. Still, he had already learned this young man could be very persistent and one way or another would accomplish his mission. He released an exasperating sigh. "You are incorrigible, Malachi Hebron. Unalterable in something you believe in." He stood in solemn meditation. *Under necessary circumstances those are good character traits, but there must be another solution.* A knock on the door interrupted his thoughts.

At his invitation, Rina stepped into the room. "Deborah Dotson to see you, Sir."

⚓⚓⚓

"No, Deborah! Absolutely not! If I were not speaking to a lady I would say you are as insane as Malachi."

Deborah sat across the desk from Mr. Washburn. She did not flinch at his refusal. "Malachi? You have seen Malachi? He has been here?"

"Yes. He was waiting for me when I arrived this morning." Mr. Washburn gave a negative headshake. "He came here with a harebrained scheme. He wanted to set a trap for Berger using himself as bait. Wild. Unheard of." Washburn put both hands on his desk and leaned toward Deborah. "And now, you. Positively, absolutely not. It is unthinkable. At least to me it is. To Malachi, his plan was brilliant. I guess you think yours is brilliant."

"Yes sir, I do," Deborah replied in a quiet but confident tone.

Moving his face a little closer to her, he asked, "Tell me, Deborah, did you two plan your little schemes together? In case I refused one, I would be sure to agree to the other."

"Oh…uh…no sir, I haven't seen Malachi. He didn't show up yesterday to escort me to the hotel after work. Neither did he come to the dining hall later. Those are our usual times for being together and sharing information."

"Then you do not know his plan? You didn't talk to him yesterday or last night?"

"No sir. He sent a note saying he could not meet me after work but would be at the dining hall later. He didn't show up which has caused me great alarm. That is not like Malachi. I know it had to be something beyond his control for him to miss both meetings. What happened? Do you know?"

"He is okay. Don't be alarmed. Met with a bit of trouble but is in full force today. Headstrong and determined. Not easily persuaded against something that he feels will get the job done."

"He will, too. That's my Malachi."

A period of silence prevailed as Mr. Washburn observed the young lady across the desk from him. He studied her carefully, noticing she did not flinch under his stare. *She appears very confident and at ease. Doesn't let her female feathers get all ruffled at a setback in her plans. Amazing that she and Malachi would come up with such similar ideas. Only her plan puts her as bait. Never. Wait until Malachi hears about this. That will definitely put an end to one plan.*

Deborah broke the silence. "Do you know where he was going from here?"

"To the chocolate factory to meet you."

"Oh, my. Mr. Pereire gave me the day off."

"Well, I am sure you will find each other. When you do, you both better give some grave thoughts and discussions as to what you are wanting to set yourselves up for."

"Will you at least consider my plan?"

Mr. Washurn followed her to the door. "Deborah, it is too risky. I cannot give my approval for you to be put in harm's way like that. When you locate Malachi, you two need to work out something less dangerous."

After closing the door behind her, he uttered, "She surely has confidence in that young man. Why shouldn't I?" He released a chuckle. "But there is no doubt, she is in love with him." He sat down at his desk and rested his head on his hands, knowing as sure as his name was Elihu Washburn he might as well give his consent.

Leaving the Embassy, Deborah went straight to the chocolate factory. Mr. Pereire gave her a surprised look when she entered. He approached her near the door. "Why Deborah, I didn't expect you today. I told you to take the day off."

Deborah smiled. "I know, Mr. Pereire, and I do appreciate it. I am looking for Malachi. Mr. Washburn said he was coming here. Have you seen him?"

"Yes. He did come to the factory. As a matter of fact, you only missed him about five minutes."

"Did he say where he was going from here?"

"To find you. He said in case you came in to tell you to go wait for him by the clock. To stay there, he will come to you."

"Gladly. If not, we may play this game of hide and seek all day."

Mr. Pereire opened the door. "You be careful, Deborah. Do not risk something that may cause you deep regret later."

With another smile, she replied, "Thanks for the warning and for caring."

Chapter 37

Malachi paced back and forth in front of the clock. He had retraced his steps over and over from the factory back to the clock and at times darted in and out of stores to see if perchance Deborah had decided to shop. Nothing. "I have been to this clock every hour on the hour and sometimes in between. I told Mr. Pereire to have her wait for me here." Staring at the massive timepiece, he watched the pendulum swing back and forth never faltering, never wavering. Seconds had turned into minutes and minutes into hours since twelve long gongs had announced the arrival of midday. Malachi was beside himself with worry. Walking away from the clock, he silently counted the three loud gongs that rang clear, echoing across the Seine River until blending with rippling waves.

⚓⚓⚓

Leaving the factory, Deborah headed to the clock. Shading her eyes and peering through the clearing of tree limbs, she hoped to get a glimpse of Malachi. The clock was still some distance away, so she took a few more steps forward but did not see him. In fact she saw no sign of movement whatsoever. An idea suddenly jolted her. She stopped walking and spun around. *I will do it. Then I will meet Malachi. It is no telling what time he will be at the clock, and I am not going to waste this day doing nothing.* Looking around she spotted a horse and open air buggy parked near a tree. The words cabbie for hire was scribbled on the side. Her mind was made up. Hurrying over to the cabbie, she asked, "Do you know where the Villa E'Lise is?"

With a French accent the young man asked, "The Villa E'Lise?"

"Yes. Do you know where it is?"

"Yes, Miss, I know where it is."

Deborah climbed upon the buggy. "Please take me there."

In a quizzical and stuttering voice the driver asked, "But…but, Miss, are you sure you want to go to the Villa E'Lise?"

"I am sure I do."

The driver didn't move. He kept staring at her as if he still did not believe she really meant what she said.

"I want to go now. Quickly, please."

The cabbie rapped the horse with the reins and the poor animal launched forward giving Deborah a slide from one side of the seat to the other. Grabbing hold of her hat that resulted in her reticule giving a hard slap to the side of her head, she grabbed the seat with her free hand and prepared for a wild ride. She was not disappointed. Swinging around curves, the buggy tilted to one side and then back again, but the cabbie never slowed down. Deborah held her breath at each bend in the road, expecting at any given moment to be slung through the atmosphere. It took every ounce of self-control she could muster up to restrain from yelling to the top of her lungs at the seemingly demented person who at the moment had her undivided attention. The cabbie turned onto a narrow road taking her farther and farther from the city. She begin to wonder if it had not been a bad decision to locate and see the Villa E'Lise for the first time without Malachi. Feeling she could not endure her adventurous ride any longer, she asked, "How much farther?"

The cabbie did not respond.

Deborah poked him on the shoulder and yelled, "How much farther?"

"Not much. Just around that bend up ahead."

Not about to go swinging around another curve, she bravely said, "Let me off here. I can walk the rest of the way." When the cabbie made no sign of stopping, she yelled. "Stop!"

He brought the buggy to an abrupt halt. "Are you sure you want off here? The Villa is still a good distance after you round the bend. If you are walking, that is."

"Positive. I will enjoy the walk up to the Villa." Deborah climbed out of the buggy and paid her fare.

"Shall I wait for you? You will need a ride back into the city."

"No, but thank you. I am not sure how long I will be."

"Okay, Miss. You really should not be out here alone, but as you wish." Another flick of the reins turned horse, buggy and driver around and back the way they came.

Deborah stood at the bend in the road where the cabbie had dropped her off. She felt an uneasy silence drape over her. It was quiet. In fact, too quiet. Trees stood as unmovable statues. Not even the slightest breeze was stirring to shake the limbs and rustle the leaves of the domineering hardwood. A chill of eerie premonition crawled up and down her spine. She shook herself in an effort to push away the unwelcome feeling, but it clung to her like a magnet to metal. Wrapping her arms around her chest as if to melt the icy fear, she saw a narrow but well kept road. Following it, she came to a red brick walk winding its way in and out among trees. Deciding to leave the main road, she followed the brick walk and continued on a winding path until coming to a clearing where the trees yielded to trimmed hedges and flowering bushes. Stopping and gazing in wonder, she breathed, "The Villa E'Lise."

Recalling the information Dinah had given her, Deborah gazed in awe at the magnificent architectural edifice. The Villa E'Lise was named after Berger's great grandmother, a very wealthy woman who spared no expense in having it built to her satisfaction. Over the years there had been a few updates but it still maintained the aroma of the early eighteenth century.

Wanting to get as close to the Villa as possible without being seen, Deborah left the brick walk and weaved her way around larger bushes trying to observe windows and exits while being alert for any comings and goings. *If I am going to work here, I need at least a little knowledge of this place beforehand. If Dinah's information is correct, Mr. Berger, you are about to hire an assistant housekeeper.* She moved a little closer to the house. The Villa seemed cold and formidable, yet there was something captivating and alluring about it. With unrelenting determination, she eased forward. Her mind was made up. "Yes. I am going to work here. I will be the bait in the trap set for Mr. Louis de Berger. Well, that is, if Malachi and Mr. Washburn will agree. No doubt I can persuade Mr. Washburn, but Malachi, that is easier said than done. It may take some doing."

Taking one more look around before leaving the premises, Deborah saw a movement at the Villa. Her better judgment said ignore it and hurry off, but she was not willing to let this opportunity slip by. Someone was walking on the terrace. It was a man. A grave warning in her brain said she better get away from there and do it quickly. She hesitated briefly weighing her options. Wanting to satisfy her curiosity was taking a big risk, still she could not force herself to leave without getting a clearer view of the man on the terrace. Easing in and out among various structures and bushes, she crept a little closer to the Villa. "He looks to be somewhere between the ages of thirty and forty," she uttered. "Wow. Could it be? It is. It is Berger."

She moved. She heard a voice. The man on the terrace was speaking. Not able to understand his words and fearing maybe he had seen her or at least had seen a movement, she ducked behind a nearby bush. Knowing she must get away from there pronto, one more quick glance at the terrace let her know she had definitely been spotted. The man was talking to two men. He was pointing in her direction.

Her thoughts were desperate. *I must get away from this place. Just anywhere but here. If only I hadn't sent the cabbie away. I had rather slide from side to side on a buggy seat and tilt to the point of being turned upside down onto the ground than to get caught in the clutches of these ruffians.* She ran frantically, without direction. She ran and she ran, not daring to look back to see if she was being followed. Fear took hold. *They will catch me. When they do, what will they do to me? Oh Malachi, if only I had waited for you.*

Having no idea how long she had been running, Deborah did not realize she had made it back to the city until a musical chime brought her to a stop. She whispered, "The clock. Malachi." She started running again toward the sound of the clock. Subconsciously she counted the gongs. Each one getting louder and clearer. As it struck the seventh hour and silenced into the darkness, she collapsed in Malachi's arms.

Chapter 38

After calming Deborah enough for her to think clearly, Malachi sat with his arm around her and listened attentively as she related in detail events of the past several hours. Lingering on the bench near the clock where they had been since she collapsed in his arms, Malachi could barely comprehend that she had done such a foolish thing. For a young lady to be alone anywhere in Paris at night was unsafe, but to go snooping around Berger's Villa day or night was bordering on obliteration. Almost completely surrounded by darkness, yet he felt no fear of threat while struggling to come to grips with the situation. The blackness was like a protective garment covering them, shielding them from unseen assailants. Words kept nudging his brain. *The night is not always your enemy. It was at night with the help of Articus, the Dotson's bull, that I outwitted the man who followed me from Pueblo to the farm. Like now,* more times than not, the night is your friend.

"Deborah…."

"Don't scold me, Malachi."

Malachi held her in a tight embrace before standing to his feet. Pushing aside any reprimand, he took her hand. "Come on. I will walk you to the hotel."

"But we are not supposed to be seen walking around Paris together after dark. During daylight hours we can pass it off as mere acquaintances."

"What we are not supposed to do is immaterial at the moment. You are not walking these dark streets by yourself. I feel no immediate danger, and the important thing is to see you safely to the Hotel d'Alsace." He pushed aside the thought that if someone had followed her and they were seen together, it would really put her in harm's way.

The hotel lobby was quiet. Malachi looked about. Nothing seemed amiss. His eyes followed Deborah up the flight of stairs that led to her room. Exiting the building, he walked a safe distance away from the street light that cast a shadowy mist over the facade of the hotel. Lingering near the edge of the darkness, he kept a watchful eye on the entrance. Seeing no movement and from all appearances there was no one lurking nearby, he walked to the corner of the building. Looking upward, he saw the window shade go up and down twice, which was Deborah's signal to him that she was safely inside her room. Satisfied that all was well, he hurried to his own accommodations at a small boarding house located on a bordering street near the hotel.

Lying in bed, he stared wide eyed into the darkness, angry with himself, with Washburn, and although he tried not to let it show, he was upset with Deborah. To be truthful, he really could not fault Mr. Washburn or himself. Deborah had taken on the responsibility to do such a wild thing. His meditations were frightening. *She was in danger simply by being on the premises, let alone her reason for being there. Have Berger or his henchmen discovered she is an American Agent? If so and they capture her, she could be beaten, killed or without a trace disappear completely from the face of the earth. I rue the day she and I came to Paris, France.* Knowing how damaging his present state of mind was, he searched for a word, a sentence or a phrase to replace the negative with the positive. Somewhere from the recesses of his brain came the words of the Irish poet, John Boyle O'Reilly. Very distinctively he voiced the words.

> "Our feet on torrents brink,
> Our eyes on the cloud afar,
> We fear the things we think,
> Instead of the things that are."

The cloud that hovered over him was black and threatening, and at the moment did not seem far away, yet it was elusive and cunning. Malachi knew he was standing on torrents brink where courage meets the edge. So profound was the impact, he sat straight up on the bed and declared. "If there is to be a trap, I will be the bait, not Deb."

When Malachi arrived at the Embassy next morning, Rina was waiting near the door and ushered him straight to Mr. Washburn's office. He stepped inside the room and froze in his tracks.

"Deborah!" Standing transfixed, he stared at her.

"Malachi, I…" She faltered. Knowing nothing she could say would fix this situation, she looked from Malachi to Mr. Washburn.

The Minister saved the moment. "Sit down, Malachi."

Malachi eased onto a chair beside Deborah, never taking his eyes off of her. An uncomfortable silence prevailed. Elihu Washburn looked from one to the other. "You are so obviously in love. Each will do anything to protect the other. Why in the world did headquarters send you two on the same assignment? Unless, of course, they don't know the relationship. Now I have a tough decision to make. Whether I want to or not. And it must be decided today."

"Mr. Washburn, please tell her she cannot be the bait in the trap to catch Berger."

After the first look when Malachi entered the room, Deborah kept her head down, averting his gaze. At his words, she lifted her eyes and spoke with surety, exemplifying more courage than she felt. "But I can do it, Malachi. I will be directly under the head housekeeper. I will have access to Mr. Berger's room every day. At times he doesn't want to eat in the dining area, so I will take his meals to him. I will be cleaning, dusting and straitening up his room. There will be times I am alone in there and will have the perfect opportunity to search for the necessary papers that will incriminate him. It is a perfect setup."

"Deb, no! A perfect setup for whom? You, beyond any doubt. Do you think a man as conniving and unscrupulous as Berger will not have someone eyeing a newcomer to his staff every minute? As my assistant and interpreter, you are not here to put your head on the chopping block. To take such a risk."

"I took the risk when I accepted this assignment," Deborah replied in a soft voice. "Malachi, I am not a china figurine to be set on a shelve to collect cobwebs and dust or glassed over in a cabinet for an occasional viewing. I am your assistant. Therefore, I take the same risk you do."

Watching the two young people sitting before him, Mr. Washburn knew they were capable of doing what they set out to do. Also, they both were just as determined. Realizing he was simply postponing the inevitable, he broke into their dialogue. "To become assistant to Berger's housekeeper would give you an advantage, Deborah. You think your plan is good. But sad to say, things don't always go as planned. In fact, under circumstances such as this, they seldom ever do." He paused and leaned forward on his desk. "Malachi, your plan is plausible, if not practical. You could be hired on at the Villa as a stable boy or handyman, and learn the habits of Berger and his attendants while waiting for the right opportunity to gain entrance to the main dwelling. However, your presence and purpose for being in Paris is well known to most and that includes the owner of the Villa E'Lise and his employees. All of them. They know you are an American Diplomat. They know you came here to deliver some very pertinent information and to act accordingly. No matter how good your disguise, you are bound to be recognized. Your plan sounds like a good one, but it really has as many holes as a sieve."

The Minister leaned back in his chair and took a deep breath. "Honestly, I do not like either plan. If I had my druthers, I'd send you both back to where you came from before you get yourselves killed. But...you were sent here to do a job and from what I've learned so far, you are determined to do it or die trying."

Malachi and Deborah waited in impatient silence as the Minister paused, took another deep breath and stared from one to the other.

"Malachi, you are headstrong and daring and from all appearances, unstoppable. I know of some of the tough spots you have been in but cleverly outwitted your adversaries. On the other hand, Deborah, although a little on the stubborn side, nevertheless, you are level headed, rational and stable. Like an...."

"An anchor?" Malachi interjected, taking her hand and holding it between both of his.

"Exactly." Washburn replied.

"She is that, for sure and for certain."

"Well, this is what I am going to do, since I do not want to make the choice. I am going to let you solve this problem between yourselves. Be wise. Don't be hoodwinked or lured by deception. Speaking of an anchor, you are both going to need one. Because believe you me, you are definitely in a rocky boat sailing on a stormy sea."

"I have been there before, Mr. Washburn," Malachi replied. "Not only literally, but I have also experienced the invisible. You can rest assured the Anchor that held me steady and calmed the inner me was just as real as the boat anchor at the bottom of the Ouachita River in Northeast, Louisiana."

Chapter 39

The moon cast a shadowy glow against dark tree trunks that stood randomly along the perimeter of the Villa E'Lise. Moonbeams appeared as mischievous elves dancing over the tips of hedges luring the two young people onward. With fingers entwined, Malachi and Deborah moved discreetly while dodging any light that would illuminate their presence on the premises. Their biggest threat came from a gadget pivoting on the top of a tower that without any definite pattern or warning would cast forth a ray from tower to earth. Malachi was familiar with the arc lamps which consisted of two carbon rods and a battery that sparked electricity between the two, producing an intense bright light. Woe be unto the unlucky person who was caught in the act of snooping around the Villa E'Lise.

"How many more times are we going to risk coming out here and getting caught before we do something?" Deborah whispered.

"Remember, Deb, no matter how many times we come together, you have always been here one more time than I. It is still hard to believe that you actually came here by yourself, without any protection and tarried until being spotted. You are an amazing girl." He snickered in the darkness. "I have always heard that a female is a most conniving creature."

Deborah released a guttural, "Huh."

"Conniving, but charming and amazing and I love...."

His words were cut short as the light from the tower struck within two feet of them. Swiftly they lurked behind a tree and waited for the ray to move on.

"When you came alone, did you see a room with a balcony?"

"I didn't. The man appeared on the terrace. I am sure he was Berger. Then the commotion started and I ran."

"Well, neither of us were able to get employment at the Villa, due to fact that we are Americans and not French, or so we were told."

"We didn't come together. Not even on the same day. Do you think someone from here has seen us together in town? Our being in Paris at the same time and applying for work at the Villa could have aroused suspicion."

"Highly possible. Therefore we must be even more discreet. This plan must work. It has to. Let me analyze it a bit further."

"In the case of an unclear situation, it has been said always figure out where the apple is going to fall before shaking the tree. Well, this is the second time we have been out here going over our well laid plan. It will work, Malachi."

Still pondering his options, Malachi did not give an immediate response.

"Let's do it now. Why delay." Deborah urged.

"All is well and good if you are harvesting apples, Deb. But we are not dealing with apples. If you misjudge the fall of an apple you can walk to where it fell and pick it up. However, we are trying to shake a criminal out of hiding. If we misjudge him, our plot could be foiled and backfire on us. Should that happen, chances are slim to none that either of us will get away from here alive. This is definitely not the status quo. Another thing, Mr. Washburn hasn't given his okay."

"Shh," Deborah whispered and nudged closer to Malachi. "I heard something."

Neither moved. They heard a crackling sound. It drew closer and closer. Feeling Deborah shiver, Malachi put his arm around her. The crackling stopped and was replaced by a crunching noise then the sounds mingled together. They both released a sigh of relief as the intruder came close enough that Malachi could have touched it.

"It's a fawn," Malachi said.

"In France, it is called a roe deer." Deborah put forth her hand, but before she could touch it the little roe leaped away and vanished into the darkness.

"Deb, I am going to ease a little closer to the Villa and determine the best place to carry out our plan."

"I am going with you."

"No. One can avoid the searching lights easier than two. Wait for me here."

With arms wrapped over her chest, Deborah squeezed herself making an effort to calm her uneasiness brought on by the spooky blackness. Tears filled her eyes as an onslaught of helplessness seized her. She could not decipher the uncertain feeling of warning. *Maybe we better not do anything tonight. I wish Malachi would hurry. I just want to get back to the hotel. What I really want is to be back in America. I want to be at Dotson Farm with Pawpaw and Mawmaw and Luke.* Hearing a crackling of leaves, she wiped tears from her eyes and cheeks with the back of her hand. Standing like a statue, she held her breath until Malachi softly whispered her name.

"Deb?"

Realizing her insides were a twisted bundle of nerves, she relaxed and wept silently in the darkness.

Then he was there with both arms wrapped around her. Feeling the trembling of her body in his embrace, he asked, "Are you all right?"

"I am. Shall we go ahead with tonight?"

Malachi released her. "No, not tonight. I feel the touch of restraint, a faint, inexplicable caution to wait."

"Why? Is something wrong?"

"Yes. No, not with our plan. Although things seem quiet at the Villa, there is something in the air. Nothing tangible, but I sense it. It's as if there are eyes peering out of every bush and from behind every tree, waiting to pounce on me like beagles on a hare."

"What are we going to do?"

"We are going to wait until that light strikes near us again and moves on, and then we are leaving here.

⚓⚓⚓

"Tonight is the night, Deb." They sat at their usual table outside the eatery where they had met many times to discuss ideas and strategies for exposing Berger. Malachi leaned forward with elbows on the small bistro table. "Mr. Washburn has agreed to the new plan. As I expected, he did so reluctantly, but I was ready for him with both barrels. So, it is on." Bursting with excitement he asked, "Are you ready?"

Deborah replied in a somewhat apprehensive tone. "I am." She hung her head hoping he did not detect her anxiety.

Malachi did not miss the worried frown on her countenance nor the trembling of her fingers as she fumbled with the drawstrings of her reticule. "Deb, give me your hand." Clasping it tightly between his own, he spoke softly, "We don't have to go through with this if you don't want to."

"What else would we do?"

"I will think of something. You just say the word."

"No. I do want to. It is a good plan. It is just, well…" She refused to look at him. "I am afraid, Malachi. When it comes right down to the facts, I am a big coward."

"You? A coward? After all we have been through together. Not hardly. Look at me, Deb." He tilted her chin with one hand, forcing her to look into his eyes. "Being afraid is not being a coward.

Sometimes it makes good sense. More important is to know when to be afraid and what to be afraid of." Removing his hand from her chin, he took a small item from his pocket and placed it in her palm.

"The anchor," Deborah said, forcing a smile.

Placing his hand over the anchor, he held hers firmly. "We are attached to an Anchor that goes beyond human ability. He is failure proof. Remember that, Deb."

Chapter 40

As twilight shadows deepened, Malachi and Deborah crept silently along the perimeter of the Villa E'Lise. Leaving the hack that Mr. Washburn arranged for them to use partially hidden among some trees, they still had another mile to cover before getting to the Villa. Alert and discreet, they varied little from the path they had marked two nights before with signs only identifiable to them. Thankful, as on previous visits, there was not a fence of any sort surrounding the main dwelling. Still they had to maneuver around trees and bushes, through areas of viny hedges that secluded it from the rest of the property and allowed privacy from those who were not permitted entrance into the private world of Louis de Berger.

"Careful, Deb," Malachi whispered, grabbing her hand.

They both ducked quickly behind a viny bush just in the nick of time before the bright light from the arc lamps illuminated their course. Hesitant to move forward, they stared with trepidation at the top of a tower from where the pivoting light sent forth a very serious warning that any intruder should steer clear of the Villa E'Lise. Fortunately on previous scouting visits, they had been able to elude the security device and escape exposure of their presence at the Villa and the ultimate thwarting of their mission. Actually, they welcomed the light that randomly shone across the premises. Otherwise, it was pitch black except for an occasional moonbeam that squeezed its ray around the edge of a cloud.

Taking a small box of matches from his pocket and a piece of paper from another, Malachi handed the matches to Deborah. "Use as many of these as is needed." He unfolded the piece of paper.

"What is that?"

"A drawing of the Villa. The outside of the building and also a diagram of the interior."

Deborah struck a match, leaned closer to him and looked at the drawing. "Wow. How did you get that?"

"Mr. Washburn's friend, Haussman, sketched it for him."

"Is Mr. Haussman a friend to Berger?"

"You had better douse that match and strike another one before you scorch your fingers."

"Ouch. Too late." She slung the match stem to the ground smashing it with her foot to distinguish the remaining glow.

"I wouldn't call Haussman and Berger friends. Mere acquaintances according to Washburn. Haussman has been to the Villa E'Lise on several occasions. Because he is rich. Berger only associates with the wealthy. He uses the less fortunate for his underhanded schemes."

Deborah struck another match, and they studied the sketch together in silence. Afterwards, Malachi traced a line with his finger explaining directions as he did so. "I am going to the right. You follow close behind. See this walk? When it is safe from the light of the arc lamp, I will take it. Follow me up to this point and wait." He pointed to a bush near the side of the walk. "I will go the rest of the way alone. I am following the walk to here, then here and then to this point…"

"But, Malachi," Deborah interrupted. "I should be closer in case you need some help."

"No, Deb. I am telling you to wait here. I won't need any help. One is safer than two. Also, getaway will be quicker. If you hear a commotion coming from the house don't wait for me. You run from this place as fast as you can."

THE ANCHOR

Deborah kept her eyes glued to the sketch so Malachi wouldn't see the fear in them. At her lack of response, he knew she was troubled and fear of losing control hushed her.

Malachi proceeded to explain his next move. "I will continue on the walk to here, follow the curve and then…" he paused, pressing harder on the sketch. "And then here." He hugged her tightly and whispered, "I love you, Deborah Dotson. Will you…."

Deborah put her fingers to his lips stopping his words. Then he was gone, leaving her in the darkness suspended between excitement and anxiety but wrapped in the assurance that he loved her, and regardless of what happened tonight, she would always love him.

Lithe as a hart, Malachi followed the walk to an outdoor winding staircase. A small lantern was attached to a support post of the covered balcony at the top of the stairs. Casting a dim stream, it offered very little light to the upper portion of the stair rail and none at the bottom. With firm resolve, he started up the winding staircase. What seemed like a bolt of lightning quickly dissembled his resoluteness, jarring him back to the abandoned house in Austin, Texas, that he had ventured into after his visit with Governor Davis. Out of curiosity, he had entered the deserted derelict only to be greeted by sticky, silky webs occupying corners and hanging from ceiling to floor. His feet felt glued to the balcony stair step as words of the silly nursery rhyme, like distant thunder, once more went roaring through his brain. *Step into my parlor said a spider to a fly. Into my parlor…into my parlor…into my parlor.* The phrase slowly vanished only to be replaced by another. *Up a winding staircase…winding staircase…winding staircase.* Like the result of anvil against metal the words echoed through his mind vibrating every brain cell.

As his eyes traveled up the winding staircase, he was seized with an overwhelming desire to rush back to Deborah and leave that place. Forcing his feet to move, he eased upward with a firm grip on the railing to steady his movements and calm his nerves. With each step the echo in his head picked up a sound like that of a deceitful serpent hissing in his ear. *Who goes up the winding stair can ne're come down again...ne're come down again...again...*

Taking the last step, he stood on the balcony as the voice changed from hissing to evil laughter drifting in and out of his mind like the tormenting buzzing of a swarm of flies. Telling himself it was only a silly poem, he grasped the door knob. It didn't turn. A small oval ornamental glass in the upper part of the door revealed light in the room. It was, however, obscured by a glazed finish designed to prevent clear vision into the private quarters of the master of the Villa. He reached into his pocket to retrieve the small knife that had been a valuable asset on many occasions. Although never picking a lock with it, he had been briefed on how it was done. Seeing a movement between the light in the room and the oval glass, he let the knife be.

Is that Berger? He is supposed to be in Versailles visiting a lady friend, according to what Haussman told Washburn. Taking a chance on being noticed by the person inside, Malachi pressed his body against the door and plastered his face to the glass, squashing his nose in the process. With a sigh of relief, he saw a female form move directly to the lantern, switch it off and leave the room, closing the door behind her. *Must have been the housekeeper. My time is now.*

Chapter 41

Removing the knife from his pocket, with a desperate effort Malachi endeavored to squeezed the narrow tip of the blade between the door frame and the lock. After several tries with no success, he returned the knife to his pocket and wandered over to the balcony railing pondering his next move. Fortunately, the stream of light from the tower stopped short of the main house. To his advantage, an area of about five feet all around the main dwelling remained in darkness other than dim light from small lanterns attached randomly to the building. Leaning over the side of the balcony, his eyes focused on the nearest window. Hoping it was an access into Berger's room, he climbed on top of the balcony guard rail where it was attached to the building. Once more his agile and slim body frame was in his favor. Cautiously, he put one foot and then the other on the narrow stone ledge. Knowing where and how to place his feet would be very critical for balance, he pressed his body against the building. Meticulously, and with more than a little dread, he eased along the edge not risking a downward glance. In the midst of threatening annihilation, he could not prevent a smile as a picture of Emile Pereire flashed before him. *If I had a body like his, I would not be able to do what I am doing.*

To his advantage, Malachi was able to grab hold of an occasional stone that jutted out due to an irregularity in pattern, yet it created a unique architectural design to the building. *So far, so good,* he thought, inching his way along the ledge. When he was close enough to reach the ornamental frame that surrounded the window, he grabbed hold of the side panel. Exerting all the energy and courage he could muster up, he took one giant stretch. With one hand on a narrow overhang above the window and the other still firmly grasping the frame, he balanced himself on the ledge below. Thankfully, it was wider than the building ledge. The fact that he could stand with feet straight and not sideways aided in not only steadying his body but also his nerves. Removing his hand from the awning, he endeavored to open the window. It would not budge. Taking a handkerchief from his pocket, with the help of his teeth, he wrapped it around his hand. Hitting the right lower portion of the pane with his knuckles, he edged to the side of the window as broken glass fell to the floor and shattered to bits. When the noise brought no reaction from inside, once more he retrieved his pocket knife and eased the blade through the opening. Moving it over then up and down until touching the hook and eye lock of the window, he slipped the blade under the hook and with downward pressure on the handle managed to remove the hook from the eye. After leaning his upper torso backward to avoid conflict with the outside window swing, he entered the room.

The dim light from the balcony cast a circular glow near the window leaving the rest of the room in darkness. Remembering the housekeeper had switched off a lantern earlier, Malachi fumbled around until feeling the lingering warmth of glass. He stood bewildered in a lighted room that was richly furnished with ornate furniture and extremely extravagant décor. Wanting to rid himself of the bitter taste in his mouth he uttered, "Disgraceful and disgusting."

With an urgency, his eyes roamed the room. A bookcase rested against one wall. Next to it was a lavish writing desk accompanied by a matching file cabinet. Knowing time was of the essence, he decided to search the cabinet for proof of Berger's illegal actions. Hurriedly he looked through folders, but to his dismay found nothing to support any allegations against the man. Turning his attention to the desk, he searched the three side drawers then eagerly pulled on two handles of a long narrow one centered just below the desk top. Locked. He eased the fine tip of the knife blade into the tiny key hole located in the center of the drawer, twisting and wiggling it around until feeling the lock release. To his disappointment, the drawer contained only a few writing pads, invitation cards, ink well and quills. He ran his hand along the sides and back of the drawer. Still nothing. *It has got to be here.*

Giving once last attempt before closing the drawer, he smoothed his hand along the top portion. He felt something. "Hmm. Feels like a very narrow slot." Bending over and trying to see what his hand had touched, to his dismay the drawer opening was too shallow. Very carefully, he slipped his hand inside the niche. His fingers touched something. Retrieving the item from its hiding place he whispered, "Aha." Quickly breaking the seal of a yellow packet, he removed the contents. In his hand, he held the names of the people Berger had swindled, with huge amounts of money written to the side of each. The second sheet named the American Railroad construction boss and a list of men who were instrumental in cheating the United States government out of thousands of dollars for their own profit.

So engrossed in reading, he did not hear the knock on the door. A voice broke into his concentration. "Who's there?"

Quickly Malachi put the papers into the packet and headed for the window. Easing back through the opening, there was no time to plan his movements. One thing for sure, he could not edge his way back along the stone ledge. There was only one way and that was to jump.

The door opened and a voice shouted. "Who are you? Come back here. What are you doing in the master's quarters?"

Just as the owner of the voice rushed to the open window, he took a giant leap and landed on a branch of the nearby tree that rendered shade to the balcony. Teetering and tottering on the narrow limb, he heard a woman scream as he lost his balance completely. Managing to hold onto the packet with one hand, he grabbed the limb with the other. With body swinging back and forth, he tried throwing his other arm over the limb which only resulted in loosening his grip on the packet. Daring a glimpse below, he watched it floating downward until settling on the ground a short distance from the tree. Suspended in limbo, his mindset offered no consolation. *Instead of my arm being a dangling participle, my whole body is swinging from a precipice of danger over a threshold of disaster.*

Knowing before long the whole place would be swamped with security guards and no telling what else, he had no time to spare. Without giving more thought to his present predicament, he let go of the limb realizing that whatever the consequences, it would be less severe than being caught swinging from the tree. Hitting the ground with a thud, he rolled over, got to his feet, picked up the packet and ran. By the time he made it to Deborah, a commotion of men shouting and dogs barking surrounded the Villa E'Lise. Without saying a word, he grabbed her hand. They had to get out of the range of the light from the arc lamp. They ran toward the hack. Getting within eye view of the rig, they changed direction at the sight of two men nosing about. They ran through high weeds, splashed over a small creek, dodged trees and dead logs. Over every obstacle and around every barrier, they held tightly to each other. Malachi clutched firmly the packet that contained the authority to put the final touch on their assignment to France.

Epilogue

Standing as near as possible to the stern of the ship, Malachi and Deborah waved goodbye to the four people on the bank of the Seine River, Mr. Washburn, Emile and Arlo Pereire and Dinah, Deborah's friend from the chocolate factory. They were persistent in their desire to see the two young people safely aboard and on their way back to America. Behind the four was the historical landmark with its remarkable pendulum at a constant swing. Seconds and minutes ticked away, an unceasing reminder to all of Paris that time stops for no one.

With her eyes still glued on the four who had vanished to nothing more than a mere speck on the horizon, Deborah spoke. "I did not know until all necessary papers for the indictment of Louis de Beger were safely placed in the hands of the American Minister that Dinah, although not knowing my reason for being in Paris, knew that I am a Government Agent. That explains why she was so kind and protective of me."

Malachi squeezed her hand in response. As they moved farther and farther away from shore, the vibrating gong echoed over water waves while the pendulum of the clock kept perfect rhythm. It was like a farewell signal that the ship moving along the Seine River and leaving Paris, France, was taking them to America and home. The pleasant zephyr drifting over the water swept over them like a refreshing summer rain. A peace neither had felt in a long while steadied their bodies and minds as the ship sailed on until there was nothing distinguishable on shore, and the chimes from the clock turned to an echo of silence.

"Are you sad to leave it behind, Deb?"
"What?"

"The clock. After all, we spent many hours by it or near it."

"Yes, we did. Waiting. Sometimes with anticipation, sometimes with worry and fright." Deborah was silent remembering times she had counted the gongs of the clock as the hours dragged by. "No. I am not sorry. Paris. Well, France can have its city of lights, so it is called, and its clock."

Putting her hand through the crook of his arm, they walked along the deck railing as the ship carried them through Normandy and pulled into the harbor at Port Le Harve.

"Look, Malachi! The SS Atlantic!"

They joined the hustle and bustle of passengers already aboard for the voyage home. "Hope I don't get thrown into the English Channel, again, and have to swim the Atlantic Ocean."

With a sudden jerk, Deborah pulled Malachi's arm. He looked at her. Color had drained from her face. She was paralyzed with fright.

"What is it, Deb?"

She pointed, trying to speak but no words came.

His eyes followed her trembling finger. A man was walking toward them with a big smile creasing his face. "It is only a man. He appears to be friendly. He's a…"

Words that wouldn't come before poured from her like water. "It is him. The man that held me when you were being thrown overboard. Don't let him near me." Deborah clung to Malachi, her face buried against his chest.

Putting his arm around her, he gazed at the man.

"Hello, Malachi. Hello, Deborah. No need to be alarmed. I am not going to touch you." The man chuckled. "And there are no immediate plans to cast either of you into the Atlantic Ocean. I am Agent Elam of the American Secret Service." He looked at Deborah, but she refused to look up. "Believe me, it was all in the big plan to get you both safely to Paris. Sorry, but that was my duty. My purpose now is to see you safely to home shores. We do not anticipate any trouble. This, too, is part of the plan."

"You mean no more snooping around in darkness or slinking into shadows?" Malachi asked.

"No." Agent Elam replied.

Deborah lifted her face from Malachi's chest. "And no more walking over and around dead bodies?"

"Well, nothing is certain, Deborah. As I said, that is the reason I am aboard. So, how about being friends. Just relax and enjoy the amenities of the liner. We still have quite a few days of sailing."

⚓⚓⚓

A brief silence prevailed at the sound of the Captain's voice. "Attention all passengers. We are nearing America. Just a few more nautical miles and this liner will be pulling into New York Harbor."

Malachi and Deborah left their place in the diner and joined the crowd rushing to the deck. Brightness of the noonday sun reflecting against surface ripples appeared as sparkling diamonds floating along the breathtaking view of the blue Atlantic Ocean. Finding a place near the railing they looked at each other. Smiling, they clasped hands. No words were needed.

As the Ocean Liner moved slowly past Bedloe Island, they were mesmerized by the beauty of the Stars and Stripes towering high and stately, blowing gently in the wind. Malachi was flooded with a vivid memory. *He was aboard the mighty Onyx gazing upward at another replicate of the awesome flag just before plunging overboard into the chilling waters of the Ouachita River.* Paraphrasing the scripture Papa had often quoted from Ecclesiastes he spoke aloud. "'Time and chance happening to us all.'"

He thought of the little old lady on the train. The man who was always lurking in the shadows. The one who held a train in place so he could get to Paris on time, and many others who helped him. Yet, he didn't even know their names. Looking at Deborah he repeated, "Time and chance."

"What are you talking about, Malachi?"

"Oh, nothing." Turning his attention back to the flag and the Island, he said, "Although small and doesn't look like much, Bedloe Island is called the Gateway to the United States. It served as a refuge during many conflicts. Like a fortress. Like an anchor."

The SS Atlantic slowed its speed easing into the channel of New York Harbor. From their places on deck they saw chains suspended over the side of the liner and caught a glimpse of two anchors moving towards the surface of the water.

Barely moving his lips, Malachi spoke as if to himself. "Time and chance. I will not let this moment in time slip by. Now is my chance."

Turning his full attention to Deborah, he removed a small item from his pocket and placed it in her hand.

"The anchor," she whispered. "Malachi, isn't it amazing that anchor was chosen for our passcode?" Holding the item between her hands, she placed it over her heart. "I know this piece of iron is not worth much, but what it represents is everything."

Malachi took both her hands, tenderly covering the anchor with his. They were unaware that the SS Atlantic was no longer moving. Everything and everybody had ceased to be. They were alone in a place where no clock was ticking, no chimes were sounding, no pendulum was swinging. For those two, time stood still.

Malachi whispered, "Yes, the anchor. It was a constant reminder that God is the Anchor that keeps my feet on the ground. But you, Deb, are the wings that keep me soaring. So, the rest of our lives let's soar together as one into the unknown tomorrows, being firmly and securely attached to the unchangeable, unmovable Anchor. Deborah Dotson, will you marry me?"

A Note from Tabbie Chamberlain

Thank you so much for reading THE ANCHOR. I hope that when circumstances of life have stolen your stability and leave you floundering on raging waters of uncertainty, this book will serve as a reminder there is still an unmovable, unalterable source. A Stronghold that you can cling to. An ANCHOR, Jesus Christ our Lord.

About the Author

Having lived in Louisiana all of her life greatly influenced the author for the setting of the Bethel Series. BETHEL, GLIMMER of HOPE and THE ANCHOR.

In 1940, Tabbie (Sharie Winborne Chamberlain) was born to Howard and Ann Winborne, in the southern farming town of Winnsboro, part of the cotton belt of Louisiana. After graduating from high school in 1958, she moved to the Lake Charles area, met and married Sam Chamberlain in 1962. Since Sam's death in 2017, Tabbie lives in Moss Bluff, a suburb of Lake Charles, Louisiana.

Milton Keynes UK
Ingram Content Group UK Ltd.
UKHW030841270924
448820UK00006B/59